Boarlander Cursed Bear

Boarlander Cursed Bear
ISBN-13: 978-1530967483
ISBN-10: 1530967481
Copyright © 2016, T. S. Joyce
First electronic publication: March 2016

T. S. Joyce
www.tsjoycewrites.wordpress.com

All Rights Are Reserved. No part of this book may be used or reproduced in any manner whatsoever without written permission, except in the case of brief quotations embodied in critical articles and reviews. The unauthorized reproduction or distribution of this copyrighted work is illegal. No part of this book may be scanned, uploaded or distributed via the Internet or any other means, electronic or print, without the author's permission.

NOTE FROM THE AUTHOR:
This book is a work of fiction. The names, characters, places, and incidents are products of the writer's imagination or have been used fictitiously and are not to be construed as real. Any resemblance to persons, living or dead, actual events, locale or organizations is entirely coincidental. The author does not have any control over and does not assume any responsibility for third-party websites or their content.

Published in the United States of America

First digital publication: March 2016
First print publication: April 2016

Editing: Corinne DeMaagd
Cover Photography: Furious Fotog
Cover Model: Dylan Horsch

Boarlander Cursed Bear

(Boarlander Bears, Book 5)

T. S. Joyce

ONE

"Shae?" a woman in a lab coat asked.

Everything hurt. With a slow blink, she forced her gaze to the gray-haired woman who stood beside the bed.

"Shae, you'll be leaving here now. Someone has…" The woman's eyes rimmed with tears. She gave the camera in the upper corner of the room a quick glance before she leaned forward and hugged Shae's shoulders. "Someone has made a great sacrifice for you."

"Why are you calling me Shae?" And why were her arms and legs tingling like they'd been asleep?

"You won't remember me," the woman said, quiet as a breath, "but I'll always remember you."

The woman helped her up and led her into a hallway. Against the walls were other women in lab coats. Some wore glasses, some were curvy, and some were tall and lanky. Some held clipboards, but all of them had twisted their hair in tight, uncomfortable-looking buns on top of their heads. Were they scientists? All wore grim expressions. Maybe they hated her.

Where was she?

Shae stumbled on her tingling legs, but the nice scientist caught her and draped Shae's arm over her shoulder. The hall stretched on forever. Shae looked behind her to the sea of emotionless faces. Why couldn't she remember anything? Even now, she struggled to recall her life a minute ago. Just sixty seconds, and her brain denied her. She reached and reached, but nothing was there.

Something massive slammed against a glass wall beside her, and she parted her lips to scream. The terrified noise stayed lodged inside her as she stared in horror at the massive silverback gorilla who slammed his fists against the thick glass. He paced away, then charged the window again and did the same thing. In the corner of his room—or cage?—there sat a young woman, naked, her knees drawn up to her chest as she watched the gorilla with disdain in her dark eyes.

"Why do you have a girl in there," Shae slurred. "She'll get hurt."

"Don't worry about them. He won't hurt her. She's his mate."

Mate, mate, mate...

As she stumbled past the window, Shae blinked and tried to hold onto the vision of the raging silverback, but already it was blurring from her mind. "I can't remember..." Anything.

"That's good. That's really good."

When a tall man stood in front of them, blocking the door, the nice scientist told him, "Move." Her voice sounded gritty and fierce.

"What if she remembers?" the man asked.

The scientist shook her head. "You and I both know she won't. We *need* him."

Him? Who was him? Shae looked down at her body. "I'm a girl."

The pair faced off, but neither answered her, so Shae spoke up louder. "I'm a..." What was she saying? She looked around the hallway—white walls, white ceiling tiles, white sneakers on white tiles.

Where was she?

The man in the lab coat moved, and the nice woman led her out. Shae frowned down at where the lady held her hand, dragging her past the door with the glowing orange exit sign over it. Outside, the wind hit her full in the face, and Shae gasped at an unexpected happiness. It smelled so good, like earth and ozone. For a moment, she closed her eyes to feel the breeze, but she lurched off balance and splashed into a deep rain puddle. It was dark, and the cracked asphalt of the parking lot was only lit by a single street lamp that flickered in the night. Dark clouds roiled above them, and beyond were thick woods whose trees swayed in the wind. The lot was empty except for a black SUV covered in raindrops.

There were two giant men pulling someone from the back. It was a boy, his face covered in a black cloth bag. He was lanky, but the lithe muscles of his arms flexed against his threadbare T-shirt as he pulled the bag off his head and shoved one of the men off him.

When his blinding silver eyes landed on Shae, she yanked her hand out of the scientist's and froze. He had mussed sandy-blond hair, and his teeth were gritted into a furious expression. He looked…familiar somehow, except for those demon eyes. Those, she didn't know at all.

"Shae!" he yelled, bolting for her.

"We should go," the scientist said, scrabbling to take Shae's hand.

"No," she whispered. She wanted to see him closer. She couldn't remember anything, but he was important.

One of the giants grabbed the boy's arm before he reached her, and now others were pouring outside from the facility behind her.

"You made a deal, boy," one of the men said.

The boy shoved him with so much force the man blasted backward and landed near the trees. The others surged forward, but the boy held up his hands and said, "Wait! I made a deal, and I'm not going back on it, I swear. My life for hers. Just...let me see her." He choked on every word, as if he had to force them past his vocal chords. "Let me say goodbye."

There were murmurings around her, all negative, but the nice scientist dragged her forward and pushed a couple of the others back.

The boy was shaking now, chest heaving, eyes so bright and intense they were hard to look at and hard to look away from at the same time. He cupped her neck and searched her face.

"It's really you," he chanted twice. "Shae, listen to me. I love you. I love you. Everything will be all right. Do you hear me? You're gonna be okay."

Shae nodded because what else could she do? He was strong, and his hand was gripping her waist now, bunching her shirt. He loved her?

She was desperate to give him something in return for the significance of this moment. He had done something, traded something. He was nice. He was helping her in some way she didn't understand. "What's your name?" she whispered.

"Stop right now," the tall man ordered. "You'll run the risk of triggering a memory later!"

The boy gave him a fiery go-to-hell look, and then his lips crashed onto Shae's. It wasn't gentle, though some long buried instinct told her he was capable of great tenderness. His teeth scraped her bottom lip, and there was a moment of pain before he was yanked backward.

"I know what you're doing, and it won't work, you little asshole," the tall man ground out. "Turning her won't save you."

The boy was struggling against the growing hoard of scientists now as Shae was dragged toward the SUV.

"No," she murmured, not ready to let him go. He was big. He was maybe the biggest thing in her life. He was her only connection to anything she could understand. "Tell me your name!"

"Don't!" the tall man yelled.

The boy was being dragged inside, but his gaze collided with hers in the moment before he disappeared.

Before he was torn from her sight, he yelled one last echoing word. "Clinton!"

As she was shoved into the back of the SUV, and her face covered with a black hood, she tried hard to hold on to Clinton. The way he'd looked so fierce yet relieved when he'd seen her. The way he'd put so much force behind his "I love you." The way his lips had felt against hers. But with each second that ticked by, her memories of him sizzled and blistered like the edges of a photograph that had been set on fire. And then there was only one memory left. His voice when he'd yelled his name.

Clinton.
Clint...
Cl...

Shae blinked hard against the darkness. Where was she?

TWO

Beck was pregnant.

Clinton scented the air around her for the hundredth time just to make sure, but he didn't make mistakes about pregnancies. He'd been trained to recognize the pregnancy hormone at eighteen, and the ability had never left him. He'd known Bash's mate, Emerson, was pregnant before she'd known, but this—Beck being with child—he hadn't expected in a million years. Her mate, Mason, was supposed to be sterile. Obviously his fuckin' boar-people lied to him.

"Clinton," Beck said, swatting at him. "Stop smelling me."

Mason shoved him in the shoulder, forcing space between him and his mate, and for a moment, Clinton considered blurting out the news. The idiots hadn't even figured it out yet, probably on account of Beck's patchy periods and all that. He could ruin it for them. Ruin Beck's moment so she wouldn't get to tell The Barrow he would be siring a little piglet sibling for her son Air-Ryder.

Instead, Clinton spat near Mason's feet and flipped him off. The old Clinton would've ruined surprises. The old Clinton was fun and didn't give a shit about anything, or anyone. New Clinton was a boring asshole just like the other Boarlanders. God, this place was quicksand.

"Stop staring at her like that!" Mason said. "You're freaking her out."

Clinton was, in fact, staring at Beck's stomach, imagining how Mason would react when she figured it out and told him. He was definitely going to cry. That old boar teared up all the damned time when Air-Ryder did anything cute. What a queef.

"What's taking so long?" Harrison ground out. His eyes were that bright blue that said he was probably going to Change and bleed someone. Good. Clinton hadn't had a good fight in two days, and his bear was restless.

"You in a hurry for another row with the boars?" Kirk asked nonchalantly from where he stood with his arm slung over his mate,

Ally's, shoulders. But his eyes were gold, and he smelled like the monster gorilla in his middle, so that fucker wasn't fooling anyone. He was just as riled up as the rest of them.

Clinton crossed his arms over his chest and tossed a glance over his shoulder at where Air-Ryder was burying a leftover brick in the middle of the gravel road. It would probably pop everyone's tires as they drove through the trailer park. Good boy. "Beck, you should take your kid inside." Both of them.

Beck tossed him a don't-tell-me-what-to-do frown. "They aren't coming to fight us. They just want to talk, and it isn't Jamison leading them anymore. It's Mason's dad."

"False. It's Mason who defeated the dominant boar, so guess who is king asshole now?" Clinton kicked at a pile of white gravel to dispel some of the tension zinging through his body. Too loud, he yelled, "Just do it, okay?"

"Enough!" Harrison said, slashing his hand through the air. "I swear to God, if you throw a tantrum right now, I'm going to break every major bone in your body. You have been a beast for weeks now."

"I've been way better than I feel like being! I want to fight all y'all anus-wagons all the time, and I haven't."

"Because you gave up fighting for whiskey," Bash said in a happy voice.

Clinton wanted to ring his neck. How could one person be so perpetually happy every single day of his life?

"Would you rather I go back to fighting?" Clinton asked.

"Nah," Bash said, rubbing his pregnant mate's round belly. "I like Drunk Clinton way better than Crazy Clinton."

Bash's mate, Emerson, stopped biting her thumbnail and moved Bash's hand over to her right side, like she was chasing the baby's movement. "It's true. Bash says all the time that Drunk Clinton is a great ninth best friend."

"Ninth?" Offended, Clinton looked around at the Boarlanders. "There are only seven Boarlanders other than me and you."

Bash grinned bigger. "Air-Ryder is my eighth best friend."

"You listed a five-year-old kid as a better friend than your own crew-mate?" Clinton narrowed his eyes at Bash's stupid smiling face and growled out, "Everyone here is an idiot but me." And then he stomped off, sat heavily on the bottom stair of Harrison and Audrey's front porch, and plotted ways to vandalize the park after everyone went to sleep tonight.

The sunlight reflected red highlights in Air-Ryder's gold hair as the boy approached, lugging a heavy rock. "Here Mister Clinton. Momma says you like to throw stuff when you're mad."

Clinton waited until Beck stopped watching them with that stupid mushy look on her face and turned back around. Then he ruffled Air-Ryder's hair and chucked the rock present as hard as he could into the woods. The sound of the stone ricocheting off a pine tree did make him feel a little better, and Air-Ryder's little giggle drew a smile from Clinton before he replaced it with his usual grimace.

The rumble of a truck engine sounded faintly in the distance. Fuckin' boars. They'd lost the boar-war bad, and yet they had begged Mason for this meeting. The Ashe Crew and Gray Backs, and hell, even the motherfuckin' dragon himself was on standby, ready for makin' bacon if the boars even breathed wrong. But still, Clinton couldn't settle the feeling that something bad was going to happen. That was an instinct that never went away—partly a product of his broken bear and partly because he was cursed.

Fear was the biggest trigger for his inner monster. The Boarlanders didn't know that, nor would they ever, because they would rag him mercilessly. *Scaredy Bear*, they would call him, but they didn't understand. They hadn't seen what he had. Hadn't felt what he had. Hadn't bled like him or mourned like him. Hadn't lost like him. They thought they understood the stakes of losing what they'd found here, but they had no idea the toll it would really take. He would burn every fucking threat to the ground to keep the Boarlanders from feeling the fear he did.

The memory of Mason bleeding out under the hands of their crew as they worked to save his life flashed across Clinton's mind. He gripped his middle, trying desperately to keep his bear inside.

"Mister Clinton?" Air-Ryder asked in a tiny voice. "You feelin' like a Change? Mason says that's okay. We can Change whenever we want here. We're safe."

We're safe. Damn it all, Clinton wished Air-Ryder could feel that his whole life. "Back up, buddy," he choked out as his bear swelled and clawed inside of him.

But now Air-Ryder was petting him like he was a Great Dane, stroking his miniature hand down Clinton's back. "You want to throw another rock?"

Clinton huffed a sound that was laughter and pain. He had to keep his shit together for the kid, but also for the crew, because the boars were coming, and he would screw up everything if he rampaged like his bear wanted.

Squatting down, Clinton linked his hands behind his head and blew out a steadying breath, and then another. And Air-Ryder petted on.

By the time the shiny black diesel truck rolled under the Boarland Mobile Park sign, Clinton felt like he could keep his skin a while longer.

Scared animals were dangerous animals. If Harrison spent a single minute in Clinton's shoes, he would see how unsalvageable he was and put his crazy ass down. And Clinton wouldn't even blame him. He was lucky to have survived so many crews.

When the truck came to a stop in front of the semi-circle of Boarlanders, an older man with wide shoulders and tired, dark eyes got out. He looked like Mason, but with thirty extra years of age and stress on him. Two other men got out, too, and flanked him. One was taller, and thinner, with blond hair and a snarl on his lips, while the other was shorter with a big barrel chest and tree trunk arms. He was the one to watch, reeking of dominance, with his eyes all psychotic-looking.

Air-Ryder slipped his hand into Beck's, and Clinton put himself between the little family and the boars. He couldn't help himself. Mason looked calm-as-you-like, but if Harrison said "go," Clinton would happily rip these douchewagons limb from limb just for funsies. They had brought war into Damon's mountains and put all the shifters here at risk, and Clinton was a proud grudge-holder. Always had been, always would be.

"Son," the older boar greeted Mason. He looked around at the others with narrowed eyes. "I gave you my word we didn't come to make trouble. Are the bodyguards really necessary?"

"Apparently," Mason said languidly. "What do you want?"

Cockface cleared his throat, then crossed his arms, flexing them like he was trying to puff up. Wouldn't work. Everyone here was a bigger monster than him. "As you know, defeating Jamison means you are the dominant boar now—"

"You aren't pissed that one of your sons killed your other son?" Clinton asked.

"No," the old brawler gritted out. "That's the way it is for our people. Someone has to win, and someone has to lose."

Clinton frowned so hard his face hurt. He dragged his gaze to Air-Ryder. He wasn't even Clinton's kid, but if anyone offed him, Clinton would kill everyone associated with his death, whether they were family or no.

"I told you your people are fucked up," Bash said.

"Agreed," Mason said. "Make this quick. Why are you here?"

"I need you to fight these two," his dad said, gesturing with two twitches of his neck to the titans behind him. "With your absence, dominant boar has gone back to me as interim, and I don't want this job. I retired for a reason. You not taking your rightful place—"

"As president of the fuck-ups," Kirk chimed in.

The old boar's eyes went dead. "You not taking your rightful place as dominant boar has thrown our people into chaos. We need a leader. I get that you aren't coming back to us, but you at least owe it to us to put things right."

"I owe you." Oooh, Mason's tone sounded dangerous as hell.

Clinton rocked forward on the balls of his feet, excitement growing in his middle. *Fight, fight, fight.*

"Yeah, Mason. You owe us. Right now we have the damned Barrow as our leader."

"He ain't a barrow," Clinton gritted out. Fuck him for calling Mason old names that weren't true.

"He is. He isn't earning enough working out here, and he's sterile—"

"Horseshit!" Clinton said, taking a menacing step toward the trio of idiots. "So let me get this straight. Your people brought war here, almost killed Mason, and now you think he owes it to you to throw this fight. Because that's what this is, right? Mason is Beast Boar. He's bigger than all those fuckers who came up here, more battle-hardened, and you want to pin these lesser boars up against him in hopes they survive and take dominant boar. Right? He almost died. Your son *almost died*. I watched him." Clinton jammed a finger at the Boarlanders. "We watched him bleed out. We held him together. We almost lost him, and maybe that don't mean shit to you, you horrible father. But I'll be good goddamned if

I'm gonna sit here and watch him throw a fight after he earned the title Beast Boar."

Mason was staring at him with a surprised expression frozen onto his face, and his annoying mouth was drawn up in a smile.

"Shut up, Mason," Clinton gritted out. "And furthermore," he said, swinging his gaze back to daddy fuckface. "He ain't a barrow, and I bet you knew that all along. What did you do, give him those two sows knowing he couldn't breed 'em?"

"Clinton," Mason warned.

"Let me guess…you had 'em on birth control?"

"Clinton!" Mason barked out, good and pissed now.

But when a flash of guilt washed over his father's eyes, Clinton knew he was right.

"You picked a favorite son, and you destroyed Mason in the process so no, he ain't fightin' to save your people from chaos, fuck you very much." Clinton raised his hand in the air. "I vote to kick the pigs off the mountain."

Bash's hand shot in the air. "I vote that, too!"

Kirk tossed up two relaxed fingers, Harrison offered daddy boar a feral smile and raised his hand, and now Beck was looking down at her belly with wide, shocked eyes. Yep, there it was. Patchy periods or no, she hadn't had one since she'd come to the trailer park. Clinton knew. He kept up with the girls' cycles, and screw whatever that said about him.

Mason stood rigid against the waning evening light, his furious gaze drifting between Clinton and his father, his chest rising with his ragged breath, his hands clenched at his sides. With a snarl of his lips, he lifted his hand in the air and muttered, "Bye, Dad."

His father ground his teeth and dared to hold Mason's blazing blue gaze for a few moments before he wised up and dropped his eyes to Mason's boots. With a quick nod of his head, he gestured for his two sidekicks to get back in the truck, and then he slid in behind the wheel. Before he left, he rolled down the window. "Mason…" He swallowed hard and shook his head for a long time before he simply said, "I'm sorry."

Mason gripped the back of his hair as he followed the truck to the welcome sign at the entrance of the trailer park. And when he paced back, his eyes were glowing like blue flames and boring into Clinton.

"What did I do?" Clinton asked.

"What did you mean? About me not being The Barrow, what did you mean?"

Clinton crossed his arms over his chest and looked off into the woods, ready to ignore the shit out of that question.

"Clinton, I swear I'm gonna Change and gut you if you don't start talking."

Clinton braved a glance at Mason's feral face, then looked into the forest again. Lifting his chin, he said, "Beck should tell you."

"I-I need to take a test to be sure," Beck rasped out, like she was having trouble forcing her words up her throat.

"No, you don't. I've smelled you for a while," Clinton said. Dragging his gaze to Mason, he murmured, "You put a little piglet in her. She's the one you were supposed to have a family with all along. Fuck those sows."

Mason's face went slack with shock, and then he inhaled a long, shaky breath as he looked at his mate. Beck was crying like a baby already, her face all crumpled, tears streaming down her rosy cheeks. Audrey and the girls were rubbing her back, and Air-Ryder was looking around confused.

Mason scooped Beck off the ground. His shoulders were shaking as he buried his face against her neck. Clinton couldn't take it. Too much happy. Too much mush and emotion, and his bear was roaring in his middle to Change and escape the pain.

He could've had this once—happiness—but his mates had only succeeded in destroying him instead.

As Beck began sobbing behind him, Clinton strode desperately for the woods.

Moments like these would never belong to him. He hated everything.

And then his ears rang with the roaring of his bear.

THREE

Alyssa Dunleavy squinted at the napkin she was doodling on and then went to work shading the eyes. She could never get the boy's face right. With a quick glance around the diner she served tables in, she reached into her pocket and pulled out the newspaper article some pro-shifter named Emerson Kane had written for the *Saratoga Hometown News*. Alyssa unfolded the paper and flattened out the wrinkles, then slid it across the beige countertop to sit right beside the picture she'd drawn of the boy from her dreams. Under the article was a photo of five guys sitting in front of a mobile home. She'd found it when she'd become interested in the upcoming shifter rights vote, and now she just couldn't get one of the bear shifters out of her head. Even through the low resolution of the photograph, the man's ferocious face looked eerily similar to the boy in her dreams. And even weirder, his name was listed under the picture with the rest of his Boarlander crew.

Clinton, just like the boy's name from her dreams.

The other server on shift, Bryce, yanked the picture from her grasp and asked, "Is this dream guy?"

With a mortified gasp, Alyssa snatched for it and missed as Bryce laughed and dangled it out of reach. Damn her stumpy legs, and double damn Bryce's giraffe stature.

"Whoa, he's fine." Bryce cocked his head and stared at her drawing sideways. "Or he would be if one of his eyes wasn't miniature."

"Okay, stop," she muttered, pulling the napkin from his fingertips with a *riiiip*. Perfect, because she planned on tearing it up anyway.

"Hey, Angie," Bryce called down the counter. "Safety First had another dream."

God, she hated that nickname. "Bryce," Alyssa gritted out, her cheeks flaming with heat.

The owner of Sparky's Diner shut the cash register and made her way toward them. Great. With one last death glare for Bryce, Alyssa smoothed out her apron with her clammy palms and plastered on a smile for Angie.

"Let me see," her boss said, hand out. She waved her fingers impatiently, so Alyssa sighed and gave her the newspaper article and her crappy drawing.

As Angie and Bryce studied the pictures, Alyssa tried to imagine it from their points of view. The picture was so grainy, and this man in the article was much older than the boy, by a decade at least. There was no way they were a match, and now they would know how crazy she was. Wincing with mortification, she made her way to the only full table and refilled a regular's coffee before he needed it. She wished it was busier, but right now was the lull, midway between lunch and dinner.

"What did your therapist say?" Angie asked, way too damn loud for comfort. The whole town already thought she was a nut-job. Small towns knew everything about everyone, and it had leaked long ago that Alyssa traveled into the city on Thursdays to visit some fancy shrink.

Clenching her teeth against the urge to pop off to her boss, Alyssa put the coffee pot back on the heater and leaned onto the counter. Quietly, she admitted, "She thinks I have these dreams to cope with my accident. She says it's my brain's way of filling in blanks because I'm not happy with the answers I've been given. It's all in my head. This boy is just..." Alyssa shook her head helplessly. "He's just a figment."

"Hmm," Bryce said, his perfect chestnut-colored eyebrow arched high. "And what do you think?"

"I don't know. I think about him way too much. I should stay in the here and now, but for some reason I keep escaping to this fantasy world I created in my head."

"Well," Angie murmured, "your doctors did say there could be permanent damage they won't ever know the full extent of. Maybe this is part of it."

"Yeah." Alyssa tried not to sound disappointed. She really did, but hearing another theory about her brain damage from her friends sucked. Her parents, doctors, and therapists already made her feel like a freak. "You're probably right. And in my dream, there is this girl named Shae, and I've never heard of anyone named Shae in my life, nor does the dream make any sense." *Smile like a normal person. Bigger.* "It's nothing."

Except she knew how she felt in those

dreams. She felt the tingling in her legs creeping through her body. Felt the wind on her face and the puddle that soaked her socks. She felt his kiss—violent and almost painful. Twice she had startled awake with her lips throbbing.

She really was crazy.

This poor guy in the paper didn't even know he was being stalked by some lunatic. She lived across the country from him in North Carolina. That man had nothing to do with her, and the dream was obviously some fucked-up, desperate attempt to make sense of her accident. Why? Because losing all her memories by getting her dumb ass lost in the woods and falling into a ravine was much less interesting than some hero-soul-mate-love-story. Clearly, she'd been watching too many of those lovey-dovey proposal videos online.

Alyssa pursed her lips and threw the ripped, scribbled napkin away. She wanted a lovey-dovey proposal. And not just the proposal, but someone who would deal with all her baggage.

"So," Bryce drawled. "Remember when you dated Kyle? And Ben?"

"God, don't remind me. I'm not the world's best girlfriend."

Bryce turned and poured himself an orange soft drink from the soda machine into one of the paper cone-cups Angie supplied for them when they wanted a refreshment on shift. "Not your fault. You lost all your memories at eighteen, and now you have ten tiny years of remembered history. And then you go and pick boys, not men, who can't handle your journey."

"Journey, huh? Both of their breakup speeches were mortifyingly similar. My exes wanted a woman who knows who she is. And frankly, they have a point."

"Oh please," Angie said, wiping down the counter with a wet rag. "You know who you are. You are Alyssa muthaflookin' Dunleavy, the best server I've ever employed—"

"Hey," Bryce complained half-heartedly from behind his orange soda mustache.

"You have no less than a dozen Employee of the Month pictures in my office—"

"Rigged," Bryce muttered.

"Bryce, I don't think you've showed up on time since you started working here," Angie said.

Bryce nodded once at Alyssa. "She has a point."

Angie continued. "You love your parents,

you're a hard worker, a great friend, and you can cook like nobody's business. And you are the shittiest scribbler I've ever met." Angie cracked a smile. "You know enough. Kyle and Ben were small-minded pickle-dicks who weren't on your level."

"Maybe this mysterious sexpot *is* your dream guy," Bryce mumbled, clicking away on his phone. "He has a profile up on bangaboarlander dot com. Listen to this. 'Clinton Fuller, age twenty-eight, nymphomaniac, giant penis, no STDs, wants tons of kids, loves to give flowers and cuddle, immediately ready for a mate, net worth—a billion dollars.' And then it has a phone number listed. And then it lists an edit to the profile that just says, 'Great ninth best friend.' Hell, he's my dream man, I'm calling him."

"Bryce! Don't!" Alyssa reached for the phone, but he was across the counter and escaped her easily as he lifted the cell to his ear.

Bryce pouted and hung up. "Straight to voicemail. Dream Guy's voice is sexy, though. All deep and growly."

Alyssa groaned and rested her head on her crossed arms on the counter. "Bryce, he isn't my dream guy."

"No STD's, Alyssa," he said through a baiting grin as he pointed to the glowing screen of his phone. "Giant penis."

"Bryce," she whined. "Why can't you be my dream guy? You accept me and my baggage."

"Because you *don't* have a giant penis. If I was straight, though, I'd put a ring on you tomorrow." He frowned. "If you stopped wearing those nerdy glasses and shaved your legs more often."

"Okay," Alyssa muttered. "Enough. I'm going to go stock the back.

"Waaait," Angie drawled. She and Bryce shared a look Alyssa didn't understand. Angie pulled up a plastic jug full of ones and fives. "We may or may not have set up a little charity for you."

"What?" Alyssa turned the full jug and read the sign taped on the side. Sure enough it read *Get Alyssa a Life Fund*. Fantastic.

"You have worked here since you were twenty, Alyssa." Angie rested her elbows on the counter. "You should've moved on a long time ago."

"You don't like me working here?"

"You know I do, and I'll be completely screwed when you leave and the bulk of the work falls on this one." Angie nudged Bryce, who looked completely unoffended. "But you haven't taken a single vacation. You went stagnant and got scared of life after that accident. You haven't gone anywhere or done anything, and it's time." Angie pulled a wad of money out of her back pocket and dumped it into the jar. "This is to help with your trip."

"Trip? What trip?"

"The one you're taking to Saratoga to figure out what it is about dream guy that has you off in la-la land all the time."

Bryce dropped a wad of money into the jar and declared, "For disposable razors."

Alyssa's throat thickened with emotion at how amazing her friends' offer was, but… "I can't take this." She fingered the lip of the plastic container. This was more money than she'd ever seen in her life. "It's way too much, and I'm not going to Saratoga."

"You have to." Bryce draped his arm over her shoulder and set his phone down. "We've already rented you one of those rustic cabins on the outskirts of town for seven days of that wilderness shit you like so much."

"I went camping one time, and it was at the local park."

Bryce shrugged. "Go for a week, meet dream guy, mark him off your list so you don't have to think what-if for the rest of your life, and then come back here and work at the diner for eternity if you want."

She couldn't do this. Couldn't. Her nickname was Safety First for a reason. She was twenty-eight years old and still got nervous talking to strangers. She didn't even go to the local bar without pepper spray, a serrated pocket knife, and at least two friends. The thought of going to a new town that was chock full of shifters was terrifying. She'd never even met one of the animal-people, and now she would what? Walk up to Clinton Fuller and ask him what he was doing in her dreams?

But Angie was right about her never taking vacation days. She worked really hard to pay for her apartment so she didn't have to live with roommates, and here Angie and Bryce were, offering her a free vacation to somewhere that had completely captured her imagination.

What if she just went and enjoyed the cabin and didn't track down Clinton Fuller? That seemed less scary, and really, she would probably enjoy a vacation once she figured out the town. Feeling reckless, she whispered, "Okay."

Bryce leaned forward and cupped his ear. "I'm sorry, I couldn't hear you."

"I said okay." She offered him and Angie a nervous smile. "I'll do it."

"And call us with updates every day," Angie said.

"Yes."

"And," Bryce added, "tell me how big Clinton Fuller's werebear dick is."

"Oh my gosh, I won't be seeing any"—gulp—"werebear dicks."

Alyssa nodded at her friends like a bobblehead to hide the terror blooming in her chest. She was really going to do this. She was really going to leave her comfortable, small-town existence, where every day was just like the last, and do something new and completely insane.

And maybe, just maybe, she would catch a glimpse of Clinton Fuller.

FOUR

"Amaretta's Manner Emporium?" Clinton muttered, reading off the pastel pink and white sign above the tiny shop. "Are you fuckin' serious?"

Beck growled, terribly if you asked him. Owls were good for screeching and hooting, not snarling. "Clinton, you are a complete disaster in public, and the radio station has asked for interviews with all of the Boarlanders, the local news, too, and I can't trust you to say one single thing that isn't offensive."

Clinton scoffed and jammed his finger behind him. "I just signed that kid's autograph!"

"You signed it *Barf McNuggets* and drew a cartoon penis with a smiley face."

Clinton shrugged. "So?"

"So that kid was seven."

Clinton gave an actual growl and relaxed against the pink—friggin' pink!—siding of the small Victorian building. "I'm not going in there so some lady old enough to fart dust can teach me which fork to eat a damn salad with."

Beck was the publicist in charge of public relations for the shifters of Damon's mountains, and yeah, he got that the shifter rights vote was coming up, but she was crazy if she thought he should be the face of her mission.

"You care more than you pretend you do," she gritted out, her light green eyes fierce.

"False. I care even less."

"Clinton, I've had this appointment booked for a week. Get inside."

He cocked his head. "Make me, bird."

Beck pressed the heels of her hands against her eyes and let off a long groan. And when she looked back up at him, her eyes were the yellow-gold of her snowy owl. Good. She should be fired up. This was stupid. Manner lessons? Please.

"I'll buy you whiskey. The good stuff."

Okay then.

Clinton made to mosey on inside, but some instinct made him freeze, his hand on the doorknob. Slowly, he turned, listening for whatever it was that had drawn his animal up. Or perhaps it was a smell. He inhaled deeply, but the wind was whipping this way and that, confusing all the scents. Feeling watched, he stepped out of the shadow of the small porch and scanned the main drag of Saratoga.

And then he saw her. Shae.

Across the street stood the ghost from his past. His first ghost. The one who had turned him into…this.

He couldn't move. Couldn't breathe.

She stood frozen except for her hair, long and black as a shiny raven's feather and curled into gentle waves. Big hazel eyes, a pert nose, full lips that had parted in shock. The last time he'd seen her, she'd worn glasses, but not today. Nothing blocked his view of her face. He knew every line, every curve.

God, she was just as beautiful as he remembered.

"Clinton?" Beck asked, concern thick in her voice.

Tight jeans with holes over her knees and black Converse sneakers, Shae held a book tight against her perky little tits. She wore a long-sleeved black sweater. Maybe she had scars to cover.

Cars passed between them, stealing her from his view.

"Clinton?"

He winced and ripped his gaze away from Shae for just a moment, and when he looked back, she was gone.

Clinton gripped his shirt over his stomach to keep his insides in place. Everything felt like it was falling apart. He let off a pained sound from his bear shredding his insides. From the hole in his heart ripping wide open again. It hadn't ever healed, but he'd done a bang-up job of taping that shit together.

He'd just imagined her. It happened all the time.

His imaginings were just a way for his cursed bear to pretend she was attainable.

****

The air was unbreathable. Alyssa forced oxygen into her lungs and clutched the book tighter to her middle in the shade of the alley. That was him. Clinton Fuller. He wasn't just some grainy photograph anymore. He'd been real. His eyes had locked on hers, the spark of recognition so identifiable. He looked different from the boy in her dreams. Older. Her age, perhaps. He had short dirty-blond hair and the same dove-gray eyes, but his face wasn't as familiar as his photograph had been. He wore facial scruff a couple shades darker than his hair, and his body was definitely different. It was October, and chilly, but his massive shoulders had pressed against his thin, navy T-shirt, and his waist had created a strong V-shape. A tattoo stretched down one arm and peeked out of the V-neck at his chest. And in dark wash jeans, his legs looked long, lean, and powerful. Holy shit. The Clinton of her dreams wasn't a boy anymore. He was a well-formed man.

"You can't be here. You should leave."

Alyssa jumped and screamed as the giant slunk into the alley. Smoothly, slowly, like a predator stalking his prey, Clinton Fuller walked around her, his eyes studying her in ways that set fire to her cheeks. He picked up a strand of her hair and sniffed it with a long inhale, then settled it back on her shoulder gently. She couldn't move with him this close. There was something wrong with him. On some chemical level, her body knew to run. It's all she wanted to do. *Trapped! I'm trapped!*

Clinton's nostrils flared, and he clenched his jaw so hard a muscle twitched under his whiskers. A soft, menacing rumble emanated from his chest, but he backed up, step by slow step, his eyes sparking with something she could only describe as hunger.

"I want to hurt you," he said. "You should leave."

"You already said that," she whispered. "Do you know me?"

Clinton's eyes narrowed to vicious slits. "Should I?"

"I…I don't know. I saw you, and I had such a strange feeling come over me. Like I've seen you before."

"Clinton!" a pretty woman called from across the street.

Alyssa jerked her gaze to the woman. "Is she your…" Alyssa swallowed hard. "Are you taken?"

"That's none of your business." Clinton's voice was deep, gravelly.

She wished she could say something to soften the fire in his eyes. "I saw you give that boy an autograph."

Clinton's eyes blazed lighter as he huffed a dark laugh. "You want an autograph?"

"No?"

Clinton was to her in three strides. He yanked the book out of her hand, pulled a pen from his back pocket, and then wrote the words *GO HOME* in handwriting so angry it ripped the page. With one last furious glare, he chucked the pen against the opposite wall of the alley and left without a second look back.

Her vision of the protective boy wavered…and then disappeared.

Clinton Fuller was no one's dream guy.

FIVE

Breathe.

Clinton sucked air into his lungs again as he blasted through town. At least his pickup was fast. Shit! Shae was here. Here! Here where he could see her, feel her, and smell her hair. Here where he was. Here to tempt him into ruining her fucking life again.

Clinton yanked his ride over onto Lake Ranch Road, pulled into the fourth house on the left, and parked around back under an old, rusted-out carport. And then he slammed his palm against the steering wheel over and over until he felt something other than the spinning sensation that was crippling him.

He'd left Beck back there, palms up and eyes disappointed as he'd sped past her. She probably thought he was a jerk for abandoning her like that, but she didn't know.

Clinton was protecting her and the baby she carried from the monster inside of him because, right now, he had so little control over that part of him. The Boarlanders were all hippy dippy in love with their animals. Idiots. The animal side wasn't some blessing in a furry disguise. It was a curse. It attracted attention that was dangerous. It made their lives complicated and sad. It put the people they cared about—the humans they cared about—in danger.

The Boarlanders loved the animals inside of them, but Clinton…he hated his.

His bear scratched and clawed, sickening Clinton by the second in his need to escape, so Clinton pulled his cell phone from the cup holder and rang someone he knew would get Beck home safe.

"Yeah?" Kong answered on the second ring.

"Are you at the sawmill?" Clinton forced the words out, but they sounded feral. Just like the monster he was. He shook his head and hated everything.

"Yeah, what's up?"

"Beck…I left Beck by that manner emporium. Can't take her home. Can you get her back to the trailer park?"

"Clinton, are you kidding me? I'm not your chauffeur. You brought Beck down here, and now you can man-up and take her back."

"Can't."

A soft, annoyed rumble rattled through the phone, but so what if the Lowlander Silverback was pissed? Clinton didn't ask for favors unless it was life or death, and he wouldn't hurt Beck. One uncontrolled Change in here, and he'd break every fine bird-bone in her body.

"Clinton, I don't know what it is that has made you like this, but man, you can't go your whole life letting everyone down." Kong sighed. "I'll take care of her."

The line went dead, and Clinton debated chucking his stupid phone into the thick woods behind the house he'd bought years ago. Kong was mistaken. Clinton could absolutely go his whole life letting everyone down. That's what he did. That's who he was.

Stupid phone. He glared at the fifty missed calls. Most of them were unknown numbers from horny women who tracked down his digits on bangaboarlander.com, but there was a dozen missed calls and voicemails in there from Willa. Freakin' Willa. She'd put his number on the website to make his life miserable, and now she'd grown a fondness for prank calling him several times a day. He didn't miss the Gray Backs.

Liar.

With a snarl, he punched the number in his phone that he'd labeled *home*. What a joke. Home was for people who could settle, and that had been ripped away from him at age sixteen.

Gritting his teeth, he lifted the cell to his ear and stared at the overgrown brush behind the house.

"Hello?" God, just the sound of Dana Dunleavy's voice brought back his entire childhood.

"It's me. Clinton."

Three heartbeats of silence passed. "What do you want?"

"Shae's here."

"What? No, she's in North Carolina."

"No, I just saw her, and she is definitely here. What the fuck, Dana? I gave you simple instructions, and you swore you could follow through."

"If this is anyone's fault, it's yours. I know you came to town in April. I know you were watching her."

Clinton snarled up his lip and barely

resisted cursing her out. He wasn't even mad at Shae's mom. He was mad at himself for being weak and getting caught at it. He lowered his voice in shame. "I just wanted to see her. Just for a few minutes."

"Well, she must've seen you or something. She didn't even mention taking time off work, and now she's across the entire country. Shoot. Her dad and I have called her a few times this week, but it sent us straight to voicemail. She probably figured we would talk her out of going."

"Probably, since that was your job."

"Oh, quit it, Clinton. I know you went through something awful, boy. I know you did. But none of that was Alyssa's fault."

Alyssa. Right. He had forgotten about her fake name because, to him, she would always be Shae.

"What do you want me to do?" Dana sounded sad. Helpless. "She's a grown woman now, Clinton, and she isn't happy with the answers we've given her. And if she's there, it's for a reason. Maybe she remembers you."

"She can't! There is nothing left in her brain to remember! I'm nothing. I'm a ghost. I'm a figment of her imagination. I'm invisible. That was the deal. Everything was erased so she could be happy."

"Yeah, and you were supposed to come for her when you got out!" Dana gasped as if she wished she could swallow those words down, but it was too late. They were out there, tightening around Clinton's throat like a hangman's noose. *You can't go your whole life letting everyone down.*

"Dana. I'm not the kid you knew. Trust me when I say this—you don't want me for your daughter." Clinton gripped the phone tighter and wished everything hadn't gotten so screwed up. "You don't want me anywhere near her."

He ended the call, slammed his head back onto the seat, and closed his eyes against the pain building at the back of his skull. It was always like this right after he resisted a Change. His bear hated him as much as he hated it.

With a growl, he shoved open his door and stumbled out of his Raptor. The earth swayed sideways. So dizzy. He squinted against the sun, too bright, and made his way through the overgrown weeds of the yard to the dilapidated house. His house, if the deed on it meant anything, but to Clinton, it would always be hers. He flinched away from the stones that lined the landscaping where he and Shae used to sit and eat popsicles when they were kids. The faint echo of their laughter bounced around his muddled mind as he stepped over a toppled garden gnome Dana had put near the sidewalk for good luck. The walkway was cracked into a spiderweb of dried grass. Clinton stepped up the sagging, creaking steps to a small porch and ripped off a couple of warnings the city taped there to piss him off. *Mow the lawn. Unlivable conditions.* No shit. No one lived here anymore except the ghost of what could have been.

He'd grown up three lots down in a trailer his parents bought so he and his dad and brothers could Change in the woods behind the house. That trailer had been hauled off long ago, but he didn't care about holding onto that. Clinton's boots echoed off the hollow wooden floors, covered in a layer of dirt and dust, as he made his way to Shae's old bedroom. He cared about this.

It was tradition to hesitate in the doorway, but not from superstition or fear of actual ghosts. It was more like being stunned by the wave of memories that always bombarded him when he took that first step into the room. He'd had his first kiss here. Felt his first tit.

Fingered her...

Clinton scrubbed his hands down his face and ambled to the center of the room. Dana and Craig had cleaned this place out when they moved to North Carolina, but they hadn't known Shae as well as he had.

The loose board whined as he pulled it up. Inside the floor was nestled a half-empty bottle of whiskey and something Clinton treasured more than anything in the world. Shae's journal.

It was one of those gaudy, glittery, girly books with cartoon kittens and butterflies. Clinton sat down, took a long, deep swig of whiskey, then opened her journal to the first page, just like he always did.

Shalene Dawn Dunleavy – age ten

A pained smile stretched his face as Clinton laid back and read the short entry about how she'd found a kitten, and her mom had helped her nurse it back to health. He remembered that cat. It didn't have a tail, and it hated everyone on the planet but Shae. She should've named it Clinton.

He couldn't do the full dance down memory lane today without losing it, so Clinton flipped the pages to the back. This was his part. This was what he used to remind himself of why he was doing this.

He unclipped the black-ink pen from the spine and scribbled today's date under his last entry, dated two weeks ago.

Broken, brawling bear. You only feel okay when you bleed someone. Something. You can't stand touch, and that would break a warm woman like her. Shae deserves better. Today, you saw her, and all you wanted to do was bite her. To Turn her so she would be able to protect herself. So you would never have to die for her again. Selfish monster. Leave her alone.

With a slow, steadying exhale, Clinton closed the journal and looked up at the cobwebs floating this way and that from the ceiling rafters.

"It's good that she's leaving." And just to remind himself why he couldn't have soft, pretty things, Clinton whispered, "I have to let this one live."

SIX

Alyssa skidded to a stop in the gravel parking lot of Moosey's Bait and Barbecue. It had taken longer than she expected to get here, but when she checked her phone, she knew she wasn't too late. Emerson Kane was active on her social media pages and had posted a picture holding a chocolate cupcake with a sparkler sticking out of it and her finger over her lips in a shushing motion. Under the picture, the caption read, *we're going to surprise Miss Kitty at work for her birthday #partylikeaboarlander*

And since Audrey was the only "kitty" in the form of a white tiger shifter, Alyssa figured they were going to Moosey's, just like the logo on Audrey's shirts in her picture posts.

And when she spotted the white Ford Raptor Clinton had sped off in the other day,

Alyssa knew her detective skills were on point. His shiny, jacked-up truck was two parking spots down and a direct contrast from her thirteen-year-old, two-door, hideously purple and rust-colored Pontiac Sunfire. She turned off the engine to stifle the screeching sound her belt and brakes made, and then she checked herself in the mirror. God, she looked terrified and pale as a ghost, but she couldn't go another night with all these questions rattling around her brain. She pinched her cheeks like she saw once on an old movie, but all it did was hurt and didn't make them look rosy at all.

She could do this.

Alyssa blew out a breath, slung her purse over her shoulder, and kicked her door open. She'd searched vacation clothes on the Internet, and it was all beachwear and sundresses, and that's what she'd packed. So here she was, in the middle of a dusty gravel parking lot, staring at a garage-like barbecue joint with a spinning pig butt on the roof that said *Jum own in*, and she was dressed in a short, black floral sundress and wedge heels that tied prettily up her calf. And she was freezing her ever-lovin' teats off. October in the mountains above Saratoga was no joke. A stiff, frosty wind lifted the hem of her dress, and as much as she wished she emulated Marilyn Monroe over an air vent, she likely looked more like a clumsy circus bear in a tutu. She wrestled the fabric back over her treasure chest. Her purse flung forward and swung like an irritating pendulum as she bunched her dress around her thighs and gave a mental curse at the pervy wind.

She stumbled on her wedges this way and that over the uneven parking lot until she was in the shadow of Moosey's, debating which of the three garage doors to enter. She'd never seen a restaurant look like a mechanic shop, but okay. At least it smelled divine.

She picked the middle, gave a nodded greeting to a man just outside who was working away by a giant smoke-cooker, and then she glided in as gracefully as she could while preventing her damned dress from playing peekaboo-hooha.

It was lunchtime, and the joint was surprisingly busy with almost every one of the long picnic tables filled with hungry patrons digging into brisket sandwiches and links of fragrant sausage. Against the back wall was her prey, though, in the form of one sexy as hell, confusing as all get out, Clinton Fuller.

He sat at a booth alone, next to a long table filled with laughing, chatting Boarlanders. Alyssa hesitated and frowned at how lonely he looked. Clinton was leaned against the wall, one knee drawn up to his chest, one leg stretched out so his dusty work boot hung off the edge of the bench seat. He was taking a long swig of a beer, his Adam's apple dipping into his muscular neck with every swallow. She almost forgot from the other day how massive and muscular he was. The tattoos down his arm made him look tough and intimidating. Scary even. His short beard hid his jaw, but his hair had been gelled and spiked up in a messy, sexy style that had her swallowing hard and rethinking her plan to come here. He was about a dozen leagues above her, and mean as sin on top of it.

But her dream...

Shouldering her purse, she wound her way through the womper-jawed tables and approached him slowly. She'd read she was supposed to do that around predator shifters.

Clinton's eyes narrowed to angry silver slits as he leveled her with a dangerous look. "What the fuck are you still doing here?"

"Clinton!" the woman he was with the other day called from the other table. She was sitting on a dark-haired behemoth's lap next to a little boy. "Manners."

Clinton growled—an actual and terrifying growl! With a put-upon sigh, he gave Alyssa an empty smile that showed way too many sharp teeth and said, "What the *hell* are you still doing here?"

"Better," the woman murmured.

Confused, Alyssa gestured to the woman. "I thought you were together. Or…" She scrunched up her nose. "Okay, I've never talked to shifters before you, and admittedly I don't know much about your culture. I'll probably say a dozen things wrong before I figure this all out, but do you and that man…share her?"

Clinton's face went slack. "Ew. No. I don't share nothin' or no one. Especially not Beck, and especially not with that pig."

"Boar," the dark-haired man ground out.

"Okay." Phew, because there was no competing with someone as pretty as her. "Um, I think we got off on the wrong foot the other day." She held out her hand for a shake. "I'm Alyssa."

"Hi, Alyssa," the Boarlanders said in unison from behind her.

The giggle died from her throat when she

looked back at Clinton, who was glaring at her hand like she was offering him a piece of dried turd-jerky. He stood gracefully to his full height and crossed his arms over his chest as he narrowed his eyes. "Lesson one. We don't like touch."

Alyssa forced herself not to flee like her instincts told her to and gestured to where Emerson Kane was making out with her mate, Bash, at the end of the next table. "They're touching."

When Clinton's chest puffed out as he shrugged, she became fascinated by his nipples, oddly shaped and drawn up tight against the thin white material of his V-neck T-shirt. A glint of metal barely shone through the threadbare fabric. Piercings?

Clinton cleared his throat, and when Alyssa wrenched her attention upward, he looked even angrier somehow. "How did you find me?"

"I tracked you down on the Internet."

"I like the way you stalk!" the black-haired, green-eyed giant, Bash, said from his spot beside Emerson.

"This is so weird," she said. "All of you are kind of famous, and I've never met famous people before. I recognize most of you from the Internet, but it's so crazy to see you in person. And you just said my name. Oh! And happy birthday, Audrey!" She shook her head to stop her rambling.

"You want more autographs?" Clinton gritted out.

Right. She was here for a reason, not to get starstruck by the Boarlanders. "No, you made your point with the first one. I thought about leaving, but my friends rented me this cabin, and I thought it would be relaxing, but it's really out in the woods and there's some animal that scratches at the door at night, and I can't sleep at all. I haven't taken a vacation in forever so I stayed and did everything this town has to offer."

"Hobo hot pool?" Kirk, the actual freakin' silverback shifter, asked.

"Yes. Twice."

"Well," Clinton murmured, "it's your own damn fault for picking Saratoga, Wyoming as your vacation destination. There ain't that much to do. Bye."

Alyssa gritted her teeth and adjusted the strap of her purse to better sit on her shoulder. "I kept your…autograph…but then I thought of something. I watched you talk to other people, and you didn't tell them to leave.

And you had this spark of recognition in your eyes when we saw each other. I feel like you know me, and I'm looking for some answers—"

"Lady, I don't know what to tell you, but I don't know you."

The alpha of the Boarlanders, Harrison, twitched a frown over at Clinton, and the motion caught her attention. The giant's eyes tightened in the corners. "What's your name again?"

"Alyssa. Alyssa Dunleavy."

"Hmm," Harrison said in a strange tone. "Dunleavy."

Quick as a bee sting, Clinton grabbed her upper arm and guided her away from the Boarlanders. "I need to talk to you outside."

"But…I'm hungry."

"Fuck, lady. Don't tell me stuff like that."

"Like what?"

"Like your needs. I ain't the one to take care of them, and you're making me feel all…" Clinton inhaled deeply and let her arm go, then led her outside.

"I make you feel all what?"

Clinton lowered his voice outside the restaurant. "You can't be here. You can't. It's not safe. My bear ain't safe, lady."

"Alyssa," she gritted out, hating the way he distanced her by calling her "lady."

Clinton shook his head and backed up a couple steps until his back was leaned against the edge of the open garage door. "You're human. My bear don't like humans. He wants to hurt them, and you're fragile with paper-thin skin—"

"I'm following you on social media," she blurted out, completely done with him making assumptions about her weaknesses.

"Well, I'm not on social media, so that's impossible."

"GrumpyBLander?"

Clinton pursed his lips into a thin line, tossed a death glare inside in Beck's general direction, and muttered, "Mother fucker."

"Sooo…you're a grizzly bear."

"Since you don't know the culture, I'll clue you in. It's rude to talk about our animals."

"Oh, okay. Are your nipples pierced?"

She reached for his chest before she could stop herself, but Clinton caught her pointer finger in a blur. "It's also rude to touch a shifter's piercings without giving a blow-job first."

"Okay, now it just feels like you're making up rules." His grip was really tight on her index finger. "You gonna pull it?" She made a soft fart sound with her tongue, and Clinton surprised her down to her bones when he snorted and cracked a slight smile before forcing his face back into a mask of indifference. He let her hand go and crossed his arms over his chest.

She positively glowed with warmth from the inside out that she'd conjured an almost smile from him. Finding her bravery, she pulled out a folded drawing from her purse and handed it to him. "I'm here because I keep having dreams about this boy, and he kind of looks like you."

Clinton's face went slack, and after a few seconds, he yanked the paper from her grasp, unfolded it none-too-gently, and scoffed. "You think I look like a wonky-eyed pedophile?" He crumpled it up in a tiny ball and chucked it at a trashcan. It bounced off the rim and onto the ground. Clinton gave her a challenging look. "Anything else, princess?"

Shocked, she stared at the wadded-up drawing on the ground. "Why are you so mean? I know I'm not a great drawer, but I spent time on that, and I was really nervous to show it to you."

Something indecipherable flashed through

the gray of Clinton's eyes for just an instant before he replaced it with disdain again. "Look, the shit is hitting the fan with my people right now. We have a big vote coming up, logging season starts in a couple weeks, I have to perform like some trained animal in a side show at the upcoming Lumberjack wars, and I'm not looking for anything with anyone. I'm not a fan of people, ladies included. What did you expect coming here? Huh? I'm not a nice or gentle person. I don't care about anyone but myself. I like being alone. I don't know you, and you don't know me, and what the fuck are you wearing? It's October! It's cold for weak-skinned little humans. I can see your goddamned goosebumps from here, and it's making me all—look, here is the reality of any kind of relationship with me, friendship or otherwise. I live in the wilderness in an old singlewide trailer with a bunch of fuck-ups. And I'm the king of the fuck-ups. I'm the worst. I hate everything. There is a reason I'm the last single on Damon's mountains, and you've come to what…scrape the bottom of the barrel? Go pester someone you actually have a shot with. Whatever you are looking for…it ain't with me."

Alyssa mirrored him, crossed her arms

over her own chest because, yes, she was really freaking cold, but it wasn't all from the chilly wind. It was from the ice in Clinton's voice, too. "All I do is work, stay busy, and try not to think too hard because most of my life is a huge dark spot and I can't find the damned light switch. And all that has come through is this dumb dream about a boy who saved me. I know how stupid it was to come here. I do. You're a stranger, and you probably have girls coming up to you all the time, but that wasn't what this was about. I just wanted to know why this boy was in my dreams, and some stupid, tiny part of me was just so desperate for answers, I thought you could give me something. Anything so I don't feel so fucking lonely with what I've gone through."

"You aren't the only one whose been hurt—"

"I didn't say I was! I'm sure you and your people have gone through more than I can even imagine. But that didn't scare me off. I thought you would have more empathy for someone like me. Clearly, I was wrong." Her eyes burned with tears, and she didn't want him to see that he'd gotten to her, so she panicked. But instead of running back to her car like a normal person, she stomped forward three steps and wrapped her arms around Clinton's waist. It was like hugging an ice sculpture.

Mortified at her brash behavior, she froze, too embarrassed to look at his face right now, too horrified by her actions to let go. Was he shaking? No, that was probably her imagination. She was the one shivering.

But Clinton was warm. So warm. Hot almost, like a heating pad against her entire torso. Clinton softened, muscle by muscle, and then he stunned her when he unfurled his arms from his chest and patted her awkwardly on the back. And when she squeezed her eyes tightly closed and hugged his impossibly taut waist even harder, he let off a shallow breath and slid his arms around her back. God, it felt so good to be hugged. Clinton pulled her tighter against him, and that's when she heard it. His heartbeat was drumming fast, like a horse running full speed on soft earth. She moved her cheek over by inches just to feel it. To feel him. So fast. So hard. How was he upright and not passing out? His hand brushed up her spine and gripped the back of her hair at the base of her neck, and when he rested his cheek softly against the top of her head, an accidental sob left her lips. This was better than any kiss she'd ever had, any embrace, any compliment. For one blinding moment, she felt okay.

And then he whispered something so terrifying into her ear, she froze against him, too scared to flee, too scared to give him her back. "I want to bite you."

She wasn't okay. She wasn't softening his heart. The desperation to connect with him had overshadowed her survival instincts.

Alyssa was nothing but prey to a monster like Clinton.

SEVEN

The vision of Shae scrambling away from him, out of his arms, was like shrapnel in his chest. Clinton huffed a pissed-off laugh. She'd tricked him into that hug at Moosey's.

That's what women did. They tricked him.

No. Not Shae. He remembered when they were fifteen, and he'd snuck into her window and spent the night with her for the first time. She hadn't tricked him into what they'd done then, and she wasn't tricking him now. She wasn't *her*. She wasn't Amber.

He slapped himself in the head a few times to get away from thoughts of his second mate. That would bring him nothing but uncontrolled Changes and pain.

The pre-dawn air was crisp and cold, and it was windier up here on top of his trailer. He liked sitting above the trailer park before everyone woke up. Before the noise. Before the disappointment he brought everyone.

Clinton wrung the small yellow T-shirt in his hands and hated himself for what he was considering. She hadn't left, and then she'd touched him. She'd hugged him. She'd split him wide open, and now he couldn't fight anymore. He couldn't leave her alone. *Selfish Monster*.

He opened the wrinkled shirt and read the black lettering. *Team Clinton.* Everyone had a support group cheering them on for the upcoming Lumberjack Wars, but not him. He had a stack of shirts Beck had given him to pass out, but they all still sat boxed up in the vacant trailer where he left all his other trash. But now he couldn't get the imaginings of Shae wearing his shirt out of his head.

Dana had been mad when he hadn't gone back for her daughter. She'd been like a mother to him once. He'd spent his youth eating dinners over at their house and going to church with them on Sunday mornings. She'd known what he was, and so had Shae's dad, and they'd still loved him. Clinton ran his hand down his beard and stared at the first rays of dawn peeking over the mountainous horizon. Going back for Shae had been all he'd thought about in that testing facility, but something had happened while he was there that had made him too dark to track down Shae when he'd escaped. He couldn't poison her. He cared about her too much to expose her to what he'd become. She would've gone right down to hell with him. She'd talked about being in the dark and not knowing where the light switch was, but he was no one's light.

But...

He'd gotten better, right? Sure, his control over his fucked-up animal was still at about thirteen percent, max, but he'd made some effort over the last year at the Boarland Mobile Park.

He'd been good. He'd stayed away, but now things were different. Shae had come looking for him. She'd been dreaming of him, sketching his likeness.

Against all odds, she remembered him.

She'd come in and blasted apart the cinder block walls he'd constructed to keep others at a distance. Now how would he tuck all his emotions away again? It had taken years the first time, and look what it did to him. He had no shot of being all right, and then this angel shows up hugging him?

Shae was his light switch. She always had

been.

Clinton jumped off his roof and landed easily on the ground, then strode for his truck, T-shirt swinging from his hand. Fighting this was pointless. She'd been his first mate. In a way, she'd been his only. He'd picked her at age ten and had thought they had their whole lives. Mom and Dad had called him "a lucky one." He was an early chooser. He was supposed to have more years to make her happy, to love her.

And then she'd been taken, and nothing had been right since.

Right now, Shae wanted some connection with him, and it made him sick to think of denying her anything. She'd already been through so much. He wanted to make her smile, but instead, he'd made her cry. Typical Clinton. He spat and yanked the door to his truck open, then blasted out of the trailer park.

Shae wasn't the only one good at Internet stalking. She'd given him enough information yesterday for him to track her down. Her friends had rented a cabin, so he'd simply poked around, marked off available cabins, and narrowed his list down to two. And then he'd seen her car parked beside one when he'd gone hunting for her. He'd watched her shadows through the window of her one-bedroom cabin last night. And no, he didn't feel guilty about being a Peeping-Clinton. He was a monster. Monsters didn't have guilt over shit like that.

It was full dawn by the time he reached her cabin. Plenty of time to get her a present. He cut the engine down the drive so he wouldn't wake her up, then stripped down to his birthday suit and let his bear rip out of his skin.

This morning, he wouldn't put those tears in his mate's eyes again.

He was going to make up for that by giving her smiles instead.

****

Alyssa swallowed the bile that clawed up the back of her throat and asked, "What is that?"

Clinton stood in the woodsy front lawn of her cabin, clad in only a pair of jeans, and from his hand dangled one very dead animal.

Clinton frowned, and in a voice that said it should be obvious, he said, "It's a present."

She pursed her lips to keep from gagging. "You...killed it?"

"Yeah." His frown deepened. "You said there was something scratching at your cabin.

It was this coyote. Now you can sleep. You're welcome."

Clinton the Monster Shifter had killed for her. She didn't know whether to be terrified or flattered. "Thank you?"

Clinton let off a snarl and spun around, then strode off for the dirt road that led off the property. "Forget it. Stupid human, you don't even know what a good present is."

"Hey!" She stomped off the porch, pulling her jacket tighter around her shoulders. "You can't just call me names and think that's okay. It's not!" How was he walking so fast? She picked up her pace to a jog. Anger blasted through her veins as she sprinted, and before she could help herself, she shoved him hard in the shoulder blades. "Take it back!"

Clinton spun and growled a feral sound, but she was good and done with his attitude, so she stomped her foot in fury and held his blazing silver gaze.

Clinton's pissed-off expression faltered, and he countered back a couple steps, looking unsure. "Fine. You aren't a human."

"That's not what I mean, and you know it. Just because I'm not used to seeing dead animals hanging from a man's bloody hand first thing in the morning doesn't make me stupid. Take. It. Back."

Clinton curled his lips back, exposing his teeth, and his gaze drifted to the woods. God, if she could ignore the carnage of his "present," he was beautiful here in the early morning light that filtered through the thick pine canopy and speckled his body in gold. His profile was rigid, angry, and his muscles were tensed, his abs flexing with each heaving breath. His tattoos were dark against his skin, and yep, there were those nipple bars on full display. She'd never seen piercings like that in the small town she'd come from, but they were sooo…Clinton. And sexy. She wanted to bite one.

"You aren't stupid," he gritted out.

Okay, she was a little surprised that being direct had actually worked. "Good monster. Now dispose of that," she said, waving her hand in the direction of the coyote, "and then come in for breakfast."

"What if I don't want—"

"*And then*, we're gonna do something fun because I hate that every encounter with you leaves this uncomfortable pit in my stomach. I'm one foot out the door at this point, and I have one day left here before I go back to my life, so why don't you shock the shit out of me and show me you aren't actually the incessant ass-hat you pretend to be."

"You cuss a lot. That's not sexy on a lady." But the fire in his eyes had dimmed, and the hint of a smile showed through his beard.

She sighed loudly. "Are you done?"

He gestured to her jeans. "At least you have actual clothes on today."

Alyssa arched her eyebrows and waited for him to wear himself out.

"And your glasses make you look like a nerd." He cast her a quick glance, then away again. "Now I'm done."

"Great. I'll start making breakfast and see you when you're cleaned up."

"Great," he muttered uncharitably, then strode off down the road again, his back muscles flexing with a sexy undulation with every powerful stride away from her.

Alyssa watched him until he disappeared around a curve behind thick brush. There was a ninety-eight percent chance he would disappear, and she'd be left with a huge breakfast-for-one, but this was his shot to push her away completely or step up. So against her better judgement, Alyssa made her way back to the cabin and started yanking groceries out of the fridge in a big enough quantity to feed a small army or, as the research she'd done online had turned up, one hungry werebear.

The rumble of a truck sounded against the quiet of the cabin, and mildly shocked that he was actually back, Alyssa brushed aside the earthy green curtains on the window above the kitchen sink. Sure enough, Clinton was getting out of his Raptor, with a wad of yellow fabric clinched in his fist. He searched the ground for something, striding through the wild-grass yard until he apparently found what he wanted. Kneeling down, he picked something up and made his way to the front door. And right before he climbed the trio of stairs in front of the porch, he lifted that animal-bright gaze to where she was spying. With a tiny squeak, Alyssa dropped the curtains.

She'd felt all brave and bold outside when she was angry with him, but now he was here, and she was really going to make him breakfast. She would actually have to attempt to carry on conversation with him, and right about now, she was feeling completely overwhelmed.

Up until the point where Clinton rudely barged in and the door banked off the wall hard enough to rattle the small cabin.

Nerves evaporating, she shook her head and went to cutting open the package of pork sausage. Clinton wouldn't be sweetened easily, but maybe the way to his grumpy-ass heart was through his belly.

His boots were ridiculously loud on the wooden floors, and as he entered the small kitchen area, she held her breath against the heaviness he brought to the air. He was right behind her now, so close she could feel his warmth.

"I like your glasses," he murmured.

Alyssa blew out a breath and turned, dared a look up at him. He was holding a yellow dandelion flower, and the milky residue at the bottom of the green stem was still welling up.

"I don't get women, never will, but I thought I was doing good getting rid of what was scaring you at nights."

The coyote. And well, it did scare her that it wasn't just a raccoon or something, but a predator trying to get in here when she was trying to sleep. In a way…a Clinton way…it was sort of sweet. But this? Alyssa plucked the flower from between his fingertips and sniffed it delicately. Even though it was a weed, it smelled floral.

"Don't mushy smile at me like that. It'll probably be the only flower you get from me." Clinton crossed his arms and glared, the yellow cloth hanging from his grasp.

"Is that for me, too?"

Clinton angled his face away, but his suspicious eyes never left her. Slowly, he handed her the fabric—a T-shirt, as it turned out. She opened it up, and through the wrinkles read aloud, "Team Clinton." Baffled, she asked, "What is this for?"

Clinton rolled his eyes to the ceiling and lowered his voice. "I'm giving them to everyone. I'll be part of the Lumberjack Wars coming up in a few days."

"And you want me to come cheer you on?"

A single dip of the chin was all she got, but damn, her insides were melting. Clinton was secret-sweet, and she made a mental note to go easier on him. This was a proud man who struggled with communication, but at least he was trying with her.

"Maybe I can spend a couple more days here." With a sigh and a silent prayer to the heavens that she wasn't making a huge mistake, she promised, "I'll be there."

Clinton uncrossed his arms and stuck his hands in his back pockets, exposing his gloriously bare torso. He shifted his weight from side to side and dropped his gaze to the floor. "Should we hug now?"

Alyssa swallowed her laugh, pursed her lips hard against her smile, and stepped across the space that separated them. Gently, she slipped her hands around his waist and rested her cheek lightly against his chest, and there it was again—that impossibly rapid beat of his heart. Maybe shifters had faster pulses.

Clinton rested his chin on top of her head, tense as if he would pull away, but instead, he growled and squeezed her.

"Too tight," she rasped out.

Clinton gentled his bear hug and saved her ribs from cracking into little pieces.

"Can I tell you something?" he asked in a low, sultry voice that made her panties instantly wet.

"Mmm hmmm," she hummed, feeling drunk.

He lowered his lips to right against her ear and held her closer. His lip brushed her lobe, and then he whispered, "You're burning the sausage."

"Oh!" Alyssa jumped out of his embrace and stirred the meat. Sure enough, it was starting to stick to the bottom of the iron skillet.

"I wish Mason was here," he said, his deep tone tinged with humor.

"The boar shifter? Why? Please don't say 'so I don't have to be alone with you.'"

"Because you're cooking his people."

"Oh my gosh! Is this offensive? I didn't know! Do you not eat pork?" She scrambled to pull the skillet off the heat but Clinton stilled her with his hand on her forearm.

He chuckled a deep, warm sound that caused a fluttering sensation in her chest. "I'm teasing. I eat sausage all the time just to piss him off."

Now her heart was the one hammering because she really thought she'd made a huge mistake. That and Clinton's hand still rested on her forearm, his touch only separated from her skin by the material of her jacket. How could something not even touching her bare skin feel hot and cold all at once? Taking quick, shallow breaths like a panicked bunny, she slowly leaned her back against his chest. Clinton dragged the lightest touch up her arm, and she cursed the jacket she was still wearing, right up until he carefully pulled it off her shoulders. And then she was cursing her sweater since Clinton could only run a light touch over where her sleeve met her wrist, just a soft brush over her tingling skin. Was she being seduced right now?

She pulled the meat off the hot coil and turned off the burner before she turned slowly in his arms, too afraid to meet his gaze if this wasn't what he wanted. Alyssa, on the other hand, had never wanted anything more than this—for him to let her in. It made no sense. He'd made it clear they were strangers, but something deep inside of her recognized him. Recognized his soul perhaps. Clinton didn't feel like a stranger. He was that comfortable feeling of coming home after a long day of work.

Hands trembling, she ran her fingertips up his bare stomach, over his chest, and then slid them behind his neck.

"I don't like touch."

His eyes were wide, panicked, and hurt slashed through her chest. She moved to give him space, but he caught her wrists and held her in place, and now it was he who wouldn't meet her gaze. "Someone hurt me." Those words, whispered so quietly, almost an inaudible admission, blazed through her mind, creating a pain that spread through her body.

"Who hurt you?"

Clinton bit his lip and shook his head for a long time.

She cupped his cheek and stilled him. "Who?"

"A mate."

Oh, she didn't like that. Possessive, protective instincts flared up in her chest. "How?"

A muscle twitched under his eye, and he murmured, "It's too soon." He took a step back, and the spell was broken.

Her palms turned to ice where his warmth left her, and she took an unintentional step toward him, chasing that comfort he'd given her. Clinton shook his head, warning her to stay put, and now he smelled like fur.

"I like touching you," she said. "It feels right, but if you can't, I understand. I'll wait until you trust me." She straightened her spine and infused steel into her voice as she promised, "I would never hurt you."

Clinton huffed a breath as an empty smile took his face, like he didn't believe a word she said. How heartbreaking that his mate had made him like this—so able to flip his emotions on and off. She hated the woman who had done this to him. Hated her with every cell in her body.

Alyssa had to know. "What happened to your mate?"

Clinton sauntered backward gracefully, looking more animal than man with the movement. "Amber? Amber's dead."

"H-how?"

Clinton leveled her with feral, angry, mercury-colored eyes. "I killed her."

EIGHT

Alyssa slammed her open palm against the countertop and pointed to him. "Don't you fuckin' do that, Clinton. Don't you try to scare me."

"I killed her," he repeated, backing toward the door, but now he looked sick, as though he would retch.

"Tell me why."

He shook his head, denying her, so she screamed, "Tell me why!"

"She was sick."

"Sick how?"

"Her body was sick. It took a year of medicine. She smelled sick, tasted sick. She was going to die, and my handlers said I needed to save her."

"Your handlers."

He showed her his teeth, and now his eyes

were almost white. "IESA wasn't the only one doin' experiments."

"No," she choked out. She wrapped her arms around her stomach as his words curdled her middle. She'd heard all about IESA and their Menagerie.

"I was a breeder, and Amber was hired. They wanted to study the bond, study how different shifters fuck, study pregnancies, birth, the shifter kids, all of it. Amber got paid a lot of money to bind my animal to her."

"You mean to force a bond?"

"Call it what you fuckin' want. I might have fought her for a while, but she was my bear's to protect, and I couldn't heal her. When she got too sick to stand, they told me I had to try and save her, so I did."

"What did you do?"

Clinton's face crumpled, and he linked his hands behind his head. He gritted his teeth and made a long, pained keening sound. "I don't want to do this. I don't want to do it." He was close to the door now.

"Don't you run. Don't you tell me this much and run."

"I bit her. I bit her. I didn't want to claim her, and she smelled sick. Tasted sick." He was repeating himself now. "The bear I gave her killed her instantly. It doesn't work on everyone. I couldn't Turn her. Not when her blood was so sick. I hated her and I loved her and I hated her and now I'm this…ugly…awful—"

"You stop it," she gritted out through her streaming tears. "You stop it right now." Alyssa ran to him and hugged him tight, wouldn't let him go, wouldn't let him run.

"Shhhh," he whispered, like she was the one who needed comfort.

What an awful thing to carry. What a fucked-up thing to happen. "Tell me fast, Clinton. Tell me how she forced the bond."

"No." He shook his head, his rough cheek rubbing against hers. Rough on soft.

"Please," she begged. This was Clinton's chance to rid himself of the load he'd been carrying. "I'm a stranger, and I'm so good with secrets. There's no risk in telling me."

He huffed a heartbroken breath. "No risk? You'll see the monster in me."

"I want to. I swear I won't run. I won't think you're a monster."

Bum-bum, bum-bum, bum-bum. His heart raced so fast against her cheek. He swallowed audibly and cupped his hand around her ear, like he didn't even want the walls to know.

"She was my first fuck, but I wasn't willing. Not the first time, or the second, or the third. Not until my bear gave in and formed some sick bond with her. I went months in a room with her, no clothes, fighting her, hating her, hating the people on the other side of the window watching us, waiting for me to breed her. Amber was older and more experienced, and she got impatient. She didn't get paid unless she put on a good show, so I was restrained and she went at me until I came. She called what she was doing to me 'love.' She said it wasn't rape because I was a man, and she always got me to come. And eventually I was broken and disgusted and angry enough that I stopped fighting. And then every time I was with her, it was out of rage—at her and at the people watching on the other side of the glass. I was missing someone from my old life, but I had to stop thinking about her. They took everything." His voice hitched. "Amber took everything, and now I can't fuck a girl without hating her."

Alyssa buried her face against Clinton's chest and squeezed her eyes tightly to stave off the sob that filled her throat. He smelled of soap, fur, and something else so deeply familiar it made her head spin. She could almost reach a memory in the dark. Almost. It was on the tip of her tongue, and the boy from her dream flashed across her mind, like he was trying to help, but nothing was there. Nothing solid. It was air and gas, not even thick enough to constitute as fog.

Clinton cupped her face gently, like if he pressed too hard against her skin, she would disintegrate. "Can I try something?" he whispered, his churning eyes so open and vulnerable.

She smiled emotionally and nodded, gripping his wrists, desperate to keep his touch. After a second of hesitation, Clinton lowered his lips to hers and sipped softly. More familiarity. Maybe this is what it felt like to find her person. Her match. Clinton felt so important. She didn't know how she knew, but he hadn't shared this story with anyone else. Only her. He trusted her, and despite the soft snarl in his throat right now, she trusted him, too.

He pressed against her mouth harder, and she gasped at how good he kissed her, as though he knew just what she liked. When Clinton's tongue brushed hers, she was done. A moan escaped her as she opened up wider and slid her hands around the back of his neck.

Clinton tensed and huffed a frantic breath, so she released his neck quickly. His lips went soft again as he swayed side to side, sidling up to her, cupping her neck. Alyssa would have to be gentle with him. She would have to be careful not to make him feel trapped, and that was okay. Some deep well of instinct told her Clinton was worth the effort.

His erection was thick and long against her belly.

Clinton ran his fingers up her shirt, and his hands shook as he pulled her sweater over her head. He huffed a long, relieved breath as he looked at her boobs, cupped snuggly in her favorite black bra. His palms hovered just over her breasts, and God, she wanted to melt against him. She wanted to press forward and settle into his hands, but pushing a man who had endured what he had wasn't right. Clinton stepped back, eyes panicked as he raked his fingers through his sandy-blond hair.

"I don't want you to hate me," she whispered.

His chest heaved with his heavy breath. "We should just make out."

An accidental smile curved her lips—he was still trying for intimacy with her. "Okay. I'd like that."

Clinton was already pulling her toward the couch, and before they'd even settled onto the cushions, his lips were on her again. He brushed a wayward strand of her hair out of her face and angled the other way, pushing his tongue into her mouth. He was blanketing her with that strange sensation of déjà vu again. She loved this, feeling normal. Since Clinton had baggage of his own, he wouldn't judge her past when she admitted everything to him. She was safe here. Safe with him. Safe to lose herself in his kiss.

She never pushed him, always let him lead, and it would have to be like that until he gave her the signal he was ready for more. But as each minute passed, lost in their own little world, connecting in a way she'd never expected, she had to work harder and harder not to touch him or pull at his jeans.

His hands were steady at first, resting on her waist, then on her ribs, her neck, the back of her hair, her ass. But he was circling, and when he finally slid his fingers up her ribs to her bra and cupped her gently, she rocked her hips. Too soon, she knew. It was just a primal reaction to a sexy, muscled-up, brash, burly, tatted up, pierced, secret sweetheart. His body was calling to hers, drawing her closer to him with every smooth movement of his lips against hers. Clinton pulled her over his lap, and they both froze. Alyssa relaxed her legs over him slowly, settling into the straddle, resting against his erection.

"Are you okay?" she asked, ready to catapult back onto the couch.

Clinton sighed a shaky breath, and then a slight smile took him. "I think I'm good. I just wanted to see." He brushed her long black hair off her shoulder and asked, "Can I see you?"

Heat shot into her cheeks, and the urge to run away was back. It was full daylight, and the cabin was well lit. But he'd exposed some very dark pieces of himself, and a part of her wanted him to see her, too.

She nodded and unsnapped the back of her bra. Eyes focused on her chest, Clinton hooked a finger between her cups and pulled slowly until the covering slid off her arms. And then he inhaled deeply and relaxed against the back of the couch, hands linked behind his head and a look on his face that made her feel beautiful. It was one of those looks that she'd waited her whole life for. One that said she was everything he wanted and needed. Emboldened by his stark approval, she slid off his lap and straightened, then unsnapped her jeans and shimmied out of them. Fighting the urge to cover her breasts, she stood there for him to drink in, clad only in her black cotton panties and hoping with all her heart that he liked the way she looked as much as she adored the way he looked.

"Come here," he rumbled low, his eyes darkening to his human gray. He wore a proud smirk and held out his hand invitingly.

Her face was raw from his beard, her legs were trembling, and her panties were soaking, but she was excited for whatever he was ready for. Her skin was flushed, on fire, ready to be ignited further by his touch. No intimacy had ever been like this—so easy and natural. She'd never felt so brave.

"Can we try something else?" he asked as she slid her palm against his.

She nodded, waiting for an uncertainty that never came.

Clinton settled her onto the couch, her back against the arm rest. And ever so gently, he pulled her knees apart. He would see how wet she was now. Mortified, Alyssa closed her eyes, but was shocked when his lips pressed onto hers, and his weight pushed her into the cushion. For a moment, his hips settled into the cradle of her thighs.

"Are you on birth control?" he asked.

"Yes," she rushed out, hope blooming in her chest.

"I probably won't…I might not be able to…"

She smiled up at him and traced the tattoo across his collarbones. "It's okay."

His arm locked on the couch beside her, he slid his other hand down the front of her panties and pushed his fingers through her wetness. "Oooooh," he moaned, rolling his eyes closed.

Clinton rested his forehead against hers and dipped his finger inside her. His hips rolled over her, and he pressed his lips to hers again. When he eased back, he said, "I feel okay."

"Me, too."

"No, I mean…feeling okay with you, doing this…it's a really big deal. I don't want to push, though. I want you to think back on this and touch yourself to it later. Not get scared away from me."

"What do you need from me?"

Clinton pulled his hand from her panties, slid away from her, and unfastened his jeans. He relaxed onto the opposite side of the couch and gave her a wicked smile as he lowered his pants enough to unsheathe his massive dick. "Touch yourself."

"Me? To…myself?"

"Tell me you haven't for another man."

"Never."

"Good. Do it for me." Clinton dragged a long stroke of his erection and flexed his hips as he let off a satisfied rumble deep in his chest.

Stalling, Alyssa took a long drag of oxygen. This was something she did in the dark of her room, not in broad daylight in front of company. *But it's Clinton. It's him.*

Clinton pulled at his long shaft again, and she couldn't take her eyes off the motion. God, he was sexy, abs flexed, thick shaft swollen and ready, the head of his cock tipped with a drop of moisture already. She could do this for him. He was right there, doing it for her.

Alyssa slipped her palm down the front of her panties and squeaked in embarrassment as she ran her finger along her folds. Clinton's fiery eyes were glued to the movement there, his look so intense his nostrils flared as he pulled another stroke, matched her pace.

"Wanna see," he said gruffly.

Okay. Be brave! Alyssa pushed her panties down her legs, then looked up at the ceiling to gather her courage before she relaxed her knees apart.

"In," Clinton begged.

He was stroking himself faster now, harder, and for a moment, she imagined how fulfilling it would be to watch him come all over his chest. How fulfilling it would be to hear him cry out and grit his teeth, eyes on her as he finished. Revved up, she touched herself again, and now Clinton's hips were jerking as he worked himself closer to release.

She dipped her finger inside of herself, and Clinton whispered, "Fuck," an instant before he was on her. He pulled her hand away and settled between her legs. "Is this okay?" he asked. "Are you okay? It's not too fast?"

He needed her spoken consent, and she got it. He'd been hurt. Abused, and he was determined to never make her feel helpless like he had.

"I want you inside of me," she said on a breath.

Clinton's lips crashed onto hers, and his teeth scraped against her bottom lip, just like the boy in her dreams had done to Shae. The sensation of familiarity was dizzying, but the second the head of his cock pushed into her, she lost her senses completely. It was just her and Clinton here together, and now he was looking right into her eyes, the panic gone from his face, and she knew she had him. All of him. Amber wasn't in his head right now. Only her—Alyssa.

Clinton's triceps bulged, and his abs flexed as he rolled his hips and slid all the way into her, deep enough to fill her and touch her clit. "Clinton," she whispered, arching her back.

He wasn't slow or methodical like some of his kisses had been. Clinton was gone, too, thrusting into her with pure power and determination. His arm snaked around her lower back, and he drew her closer. He wasn't pulling all the way out, but staying deep, pumping his hips just right to hit her clit over and over, faster and faster. God, he felt so good inside of her.

Orgasm crashed through her, and she was careful not to claw up his back like she wanted too, just in case that was a trigger for him. Clinton grunted and bucked into her faster, then froze and gritted out a long, sexy snarl as his dick throbbed inside of her. Pulses of warm seed filled her as he thrust into her erratically, encouraging more of her own aftershocks.

Clinton buried his face against her neck and murmured in a desperate voice, "I missed you. I missed you so bad."

And she got it. She'd been waiting her whole life for someone like him to come along, too. She'd missed out on every other moment like this with her exes because they weren't special. They weren't Clinton. They weren't her match.

And as he relaxed and slowed his pace, took his time drawing another orgasm from her, the words he'd chanted were so perfect. They felt so right.

She laid a gentle kiss on his neck and whispered, "I missed you, too."

NINE

The silence was beautiful as Clinton pulled his shirt on and smoothed it over his stomach. For the first time in as long as he could remember, his bear wasn't snarling and ripping at him, begging to fight, begging to brawl. His mouth ticked up in another smile, and he reveled in how good that felt.

Being with Shae wasn't the anger fucking he'd done with Amber. There wasn't hatred or fear, or wishing the drugs were out of his system so he could Change and protect himself from what was happening. With Shae, it was so natural. So good. He felt...happy.

She hummed under her breath as she made biscuits and sausage gravy from scratch. He'd tried to help, but she'd waved him to the table and told him she wanted to cook for him.

He loved her.

That thought drew him up short and banished the smile from his lips. Loved her? What a terrifying thought. Love meant pain. Maybe not in the beginning, but love always ended up the same. Broken. Was he even capable of that emotion anymore? Maybe.

He couldn't believe what she'd done for him. She would never know the full extent, but he'd never made love before. He'd only fucked. And in her arms, he'd been safe. No one was watching, no one was judging, and Shae had worn that look in her eyes that said that deep down inside of her memories, he was still there. Her childhood love. The Clinton he wished he still was. The only place the unbroken side of him lived was in her mind, and there was something beautiful about that. He liked the thought of Shae protecting the boy he'd been.

He should tell her who she was.

Ticking a sound behind his teeth, he fought the urge to flip the table and hated himself just for thinking about telling her the truth. If she found out how royally she'd been lied to, by her parents, by him, she would leave and never come back. And now that wasn't acceptable anymore. Not after what they'd done together. She didn't know because she was human and didn't have his animal instincts, but she'd bonded them better than Amber had ever managed. Or maybe he'd never broken the bond with Shae like he'd thought. Maybe the bond had been sitting in his shredded heart all these years, waiting to be strengthened by her healing touch again.

My mate.

Clinton pulled at the neck of his T-shirt to make it easier to breathe. She would need more time. He had to be a patient hunter if he was going to convince her to stay with a fuck-up like him. She'd fallen in love with the good Clinton all those years ago. She didn't know him now. Would be disappointed in how far he'd fallen. In how weak he'd become. She would see him act out in an effort to keep his bear steady and would see the disappointment in the Boarlanders' eyes. She would watch him spiral, because that's what he did. And a woman like Shae wouldn't put up with the shit he pulled. He had to figure out how to get better, fast. He had to show her he could be good again someday if only she would stay and push him in the right direction. If only she would stay and stitch his fucked-up, shattered heart back together one tattered piece at a time.

She could banish Amber and all her poison from his mind if only Shae would stay here with him.

He'd hated women for a while, and he hadn't wanted them at the trailer parks where he'd lived. He'd bounced from crew to crew avoiding the couplings, and now, after a few days back in Shae's presence, he wanted to draw up and face the world to keep her safe again. He wanted her close where he could protect her. Where he could adore her. Where he could see the smiles on her face and hope he'd caused them.

"Can you meet my crew?" he asked, feeling like a jackass for what he was really asking. Shae still deserved better, but maybe someday, if he worked long enough, and hard enough, he could give her a happy life.

"I met them yesterday," she said in a happy tinkling voice. It was so strange comparing her to the girl she used to be. Shae had changed completely in some ways, but was utterly the same in others. It was fun peeling back her layers now.

"I mean, I don't want you to leave, so maybe could you meet with my alpha."

Shae pulled the pan of gravy from the burner and frowned over her shoulder at him.

"For what?"

Just say it you coward. "I don't want you to go. I want you to meet with Harrison so I can ask him if you can stay in ten-ten."

"What's ten-ten?"

"An old singlewide trailer. It's special, though. The mates have all stayed there. Bash swears it's magic. Good luck and all that shit."

"The mates?"

Oh, right. "The girlfriends and wives. They're called mates."

"O-oh." Shae blinked those big, gorgeous hazel eyes, then turned away from him, back to her work at the stove. He hadn't missed it, though—the smile right before she'd hidden her face from him. "That would be okay. I can ask my boss for a few more days off."

"Okay." But in a few days, he was going to ask her to stay a few more, and a few more after that, and then forever. For Shae, this would all be fast, but for him, he'd been hers since he was ten.

"I should tell you something."

There was darkness in her voice and he wanted to kiss her, make her feel better. "Tell me anything." *I mean, goddamn, she absorbed your secrets and went straight to healing you.* Shae could tell him she was a bucktoothed cannibal were-gopher, and it would only make him like her more.

"I had an accident…"

Oh shit, here it was, and now he felt like grit.

"I was eighteen, and I got lost in the woods. Fell down some big ravine and hit my head. I was in a coma for a while, and when I woke up, I couldn't remember anything from before. Nothing." She cast him a quick glance over her shoulder, and that helpless expression drew him to her.

Clinton approached her slowly, then slipped his arms around her waist from behind and rested his chin on her shoulder.

"So, I had a really hard time after that. I didn't remember my parents or any of my friends from before. I remembered how to read, talk and walk, and all of the things I needed to function, but everything else was just gone. Just…poof."

She laughed out the saddest sound, and it gutted Clinton. It had been his idea to lie, his idea for her parents to give her a new name and a new life far away from here, just in case the International Exchange of Shifter Studies reneged on their deal and came after her again. Hell, it had been his fault she'd been taken in the first place.

"So anyway, I've had trouble holding down relationships because I just don't have that much history. I have no memory of my childhood. I woke up at nineteen, three weeks after my birthday, and I was a blank slate."

"That's okay with me."

"You say that now—"

"I'll say it always. It's okay."

She blew out a shaky breath, and her shoulders relaxed. "I like the way you handled it."

Crap, was he too flippant? "What do you mean?"

"I mean, most of the time when I admit that to someone, they don't know what to say and get really uncomfortable, but you just, I don't know. You just took it in stride and were okay with it. So, thanks for that."

Her cheeks swelled with a smile, and he nuzzled his beard against her neck, drawing a breathy giggle from her lips. The sound settled his snarling bear.

Growing serious as she made two plates, he swore, "I won't ever let you get lost in the woods again."

Shae didn't know the full extent of his oath. She didn't know that it was his declaration he would never let harm come to her again. He would never let IESS or IESA or this damned shifter rights vote hurt her. She'd been through enough.

They both had.

TEN

"I was supposed to get a pedicure today and get a massage."

Clinton turned from where he was washing his hands in the en suite bathroom and offered her a horrified look. "Why would you want a stranger touching you?"

"Well, I don't. I'm setting it up for you to paint my nails and give me a back massage," she teased.

Clinton ran and leapt through the air, and Alyssa screamed as he landed on his hands and knees, straddling her on the bed. "I've never painted a nail in my life, but I would be fucking awesome at it. I'm awesome at everything."

"Cocky."

"I have a big cocky, too."

Alyssa groaned, but the sound turned to

giggles as Clinton tickled her ribs. "Stop! I was comfortable!"

"Are we spending the entire day in bed? I've never done that before." Clinton was practically humming for some kind of action, and it was plain and clear to Alyssa he wasn't the type of man to sit around. He got bored too easily. Clinton lifted off her in a perfect plank, his muscles bulging everywhere, tattoos on display, nipple bars looking so damn bitable. "Where is your nail polish?"

"Really?"

Clinton nodded. "Tell me quick before I change my mind."

"In that floral bag on the sink," she rushed out. As he slid off the bed and sauntered into the bathroom, she told him, "I've never had a man paint my toes."

"Have you had boyfriends?" he asked in a careful tone.

"In my whole life?" Because she didn't know the answer for her first eighteen years.

"No, just that you remember."

"Yes. Two. They both lived in my hometown. Kyle was a bank teller, and Ben owned a coffee shop."

Clinton growled. "What color do you want?"

"You pick. Whatever you think would look pretty on me."

"Well, that narrows it down to every color on the spectrum." He meandered back into the bedroom with a slight frown marring his blond brows, and he wouldn't meet her gaze again. "What were their names?"

"Who?"

"Your ex boyfriends."

"I told you, Kyle and Ben."

"No, I mean their last names."

She shook her head and laughed. "Oh no. I'm not talking about them anymore. It's about us now, and if I tell you their last names, I'm gonna be real disappointed in you if they end up in a ditch somewhere." She was mostly teasing. He probably wouldn't actually go find them.

"Fine," he muttered, unscrewing the cap on some fire-engine red nail polish. "Oh, my God, your toes are so fuckin' cute." He plopped down on his side and drew her leg over his waist. "I always loved how they were in a perfect diagonal line." He brushed his fingertip over the top of her toes.

Alyssa put an extra pillow under her head and frowned at him. "What do you mean you always loved them?"

But Clinton was apparently very busy painting her toenails now because he didn't answer.

"Clinton, what did you mean?"

"I mean from the first day I saw you in Saratoga, you were wearing flip-flops, for reasons I can't fathom, because it's cold as a witch's tit up here, but I noticed your toes." His voice dipped to a grumpy snarl. "And I liked them."

"Oh." She let him work for a while before she asked, "Can I tell you the dream I had about the boy who looks like you?"

"I wish you would leave it alone."

"You're being rude again."

Clinton blew on her toes and then tossed her a bright-eyed glare. "I ain't him, and he ain't me. I don't want to hear about this boy who has nothing to do with me. You can like me as I am or not."

"Oh, Clinton. That's not what I was saying at all. I'm sorry if you think I'm trying to mash you up with some idealistic image I have in my head. I'm not. I like you the way you are."

Clinton snorted. "You would be the only one."

She canted her head on the pillow and watched him paint the big toe of her other foot. He was so gentle and precise, like he wanted it to be perfect for her. "What do you mean?"

"I'm the resident screw-up at the trailer park, really of all of Damon's mountains. I'm on a C-Team crew, and even my own people call me Crazy Clinton, and they ain't wrong. When I talked to my mom a few months ago, she told me she doesn't understand how I got this way. She said she doesn't even recognize me anymore."

Alyssa reached down and brushed her fingertips over his elbow. Clinton tensed but allowed the affection. "Were you two close?"

"Yeah. I was close with both my parents. But I made a decision when I was sixteen that they hated, and when I came out of that decision, I wasn't their little boy anymore. And I guess that still makes my mom really angry. And I get it. I would be pissed at my kid, too."

"What decision?"

Clinton shook his head for a long time, then blew on her other foot. "It was just something I had to do if I was going to have a shot at being happy again."

"Do you know a girl named Shae?" Alyssa blurted out. Because what he was saying seemed so familiar, like maybe she had a supernatural connection with this girl in her dream.

Clinton went rigid, then slowly leveled her with an angry look. "No, and if this is something to do with your dream, I told you, that ain't me. You have to let that go."

"But, I can't."

"But you have to!" Clinton rocked off the bed and strode into the bathroom again.

She'd pissed him off. Something about her dream made him angry, but that wasn't fair. "So," she drawled, stepping carefully off the bed so she didn't mess up her nails, "you're allowed to have baggage, but I can't? You don't want to deal with me, is that it? Because I've done this before with Ben and Kyle, and this is just like what always happens, except at least they were nice enough to wait a few months before they bolted."

"Don't compare me to those assholes," Clinton gritted out, brushing past her. "They weren't worthy of you. You picked bad. That had nothing to do with me."

"But you're shutting me down—"

"Because it hurts!" Clinton backed into the kitchen and she followed. In a softer voice, he said, "It hurts to talk about some boy you obviously have a connection with. I want to be it for you now. Me. Not anyone else. Not your exes. Not that boy from your dreams. *I* will give anything to protect you, *I* will give anything to see you happy, *I* will be the one breathing for your smile, and all those ghosts you keep bringing up are pitting me against people who have no substance! I want you to see me." He gripped his shirt right over his chest. "*Me*. I thought my biggest competition would be myself. I'm a hundred percent guaranteed to screw this up on my own. I don't want others in your head. One minute I think I can do this, and I think I can get better, work hard, and make you happy, but not if I'm dragging ghosts, too! I don't want to be compared to anyone else. I'm worse. I already lose, and I'm really fuckin' tired of losing."

"Okay." Feeling like crap, she murmured, "You're right. I wasn't thinking about your feelings. When you were talking about Amber, I hated her, and it made me angry. You weren't mean enough to compare me to her, and I just did that with two people. It was messed up, and I'm sorry."

Clinton eyed her suspiciously. "You don't have to apologize."

"Well, that's what you do when you're wrong. You apologize, and I was wrong. I *am* sorry. And…" She looked down at her perfectly painted toes. "You did a really good job on my pedicure."

"I told you I was good at everything." But the cockiness had gone, and in its place was a tinge of humor. "Did we just have our first fight?"

"Clinton Fuller, I think we've been in one long fight since I laid eyes on you." He was letting her in, but on his own terms. This was his language—combativeness, defensiveness, pride. She'd never met anyone so complicated, but that was part of the fun with Clinton.

After one argument, she knew so much more about him than maybe she knew anyone. He might sound overconfident, but he'd just exposed his insecurities. He'd just told her he was in this, but she had to go easy on him until he could find his footing.

What a mess Clinton was.

What a mysterious, complicated, *beautiful* mess.

ELEVEN

Clinton surprised her by slipping his big, calloused hand over her thigh. The butterflies went to flapping in her stomach so hard she tensed her muscles and swallowed a happy squeak. How did he do this to her? How did he get such a reaction from her body with a simple touch? She was the fuse of a firecracker waiting to be lit, and he was the damned match.

"Is this okay?" he asked low, gray eyes worried as he dared to take his attention off the road for a second.

She pursed her lips to stifle her smile because it was a very serious question to him. Clinton—stompy, brash, mouthy, dominant Clinton—was making sure he was allowed to touch her. The smile slipped from her lips. His consideration reflected how deeply Amber had hurt him that he was this careful with consent for any kind of intimacy.

Someday, she wanted to know everything. She wanted to know about his first time, the pain, the insecurities, and the long-term damage it had done to him. With God as her witness, she swore she would make his life easier. She wanted to shoulder the burden of that pain. But right now, she didn't know if she could be strong enough to ask the questions and hear the answers without falling apart. Clinton deserved strong support. He deserved a listening ear and gentle hugs, not her tears, not having to console her when he was the one who'd lived through it.

She needed to be better for him. Braver and stronger. Clinton deserved someone in his life who was stable, and capable of propping him up when he was weak.

"Clinton," she said, turning her shoulders toward him and curling her legs onto the passenger's seat. She lifted his hand to her lips and kissed his knuckles softly before she rested his palm back on her thigh. "You can touch me how you like. I love that you make sure I'm okay, but here's what you do to me when you touch me. I get this beautiful breathless feeling, and I get so happy. I feel warm and safe, and sometimes when you brush my arm or my leg, you get this little smile, and it's so…" Perfect, heart stopping, dashing.

"So what?" Clinton asked over the soft drone of the radio.

"It's hard to explain. It's like going to the store and an old friend taps you on the shoulder. You turn around and realize how much you've missed them, how happy you are to see them right there in that moment." She swallowed hard and rested her cheek against the seat. "Your smile feels like home."

Clinton exhaled a shaky breath before flashing her that smile again. The one where just the corners of his mouth curved up slightly. He didn't do huge grins yet, but he would, and when he did, she knew he would be stunning.

"I like the way you say things," he said low.

She crossed her eyes and puffed her cheeks out in a silly face, and his smile reached his eyes. He lifted her wrist to his lips and let them linger there, right over her pulse.

God, he was handsome. T-shirt clinging to his defined chest, one arm draped over the wheel as he drove them to his trailer park, the sunlight streaming through the window, hitting his eyes just right. They were a darker gray now, which told her his bear was content. And even though she hadn't met his animal yet, she already loved him, because he was a part of Clinton. Alyssa had fallen so hard. This wasn't like her. She wasn't Safety First anymore. She wasn't the responsible one. Now she was Adventuresome Alyssa, because Clinton brought something out in her that wanted to live. That wanted to take risks and shake things up. He made her feel daring, and for the first time since she could remember, she was excited her days here weren't planned out and identical to the ones before.

She wasn't ready to go back home.

Her attention drifted to the towering pine trees that lined the road and blurred by. The landscape suddenly turned to a clearing, and what she saw there had her gasping and leaning forward in her seat. Clinton tossed her a worried look, but slowed and pulled over to the side of the road.

The entire clearing was scorched, the earth blackened. "Is this…?"

"Yes." Clinton's gaze drifted to the burned wreckage. "This is where IESA made their last move. They tried to kill Kirk's mate, Ally, so it would start a war with the shifters. Her death was meant to unify humans against us. She got hurt. Has a limp now from chemical burns. I see Kirk watching her walk sometimes, and his eyes go all wrecked. He almost didn't get her out of there."

"I saw on the news that some of the shifters here were fighting the fire."

"I was there. They used accelerant during a hot month, and it could've taken every inch of Damon's mountains. All three trailer parks, Asheland, Grayland, Boarland. Mates. Kids. IESA put everything we've built here at risk, but that's what they've always done. Too many mates got the government's attention. I used to be so fuckin' scared of attention on this place. I didn't want humans taking notice of the pairings here. Of the babies. We were safer when it was just a few bachelor groups."

"You didn't want women up here?"

"Hell no. Women bring trouble. Bring pain. I wanted my friends to be safe. *I* wanted to be safe."

Shit. "Because you were a breeder?"

Clinton just stared out the window at the scorched earth, his only movement a small muscle that jumped in his jaw.

"How long?"

Clinton offered her the empty smile she

hated—the plastered one he used to shut down. "Two years. I escaped when I was twenty. After I killed Amber, I wasn't safe to be paired with another mate. Maybe they were going to put me down, I don't know, but one of the observers decided she was going to *save* me. Our handlers never wore nametags, but she told me her name was Alice. So she snuck me out one night, and drove me across a state border. I still don't know why she did it. When I was in there, she'd been the meanest. The most brutal. Maybe she had to turn off her humanity to do a job like that. And I remember in the car, she was crying. Just tears rollin' down her face, and I asked why she'd done it. And she said she'd seen enough. That she couldn't watch it anymore. I asked why she was crying over someone like me, and she said she wasn't. She said she was crying because they would kill her for destroying their program. She'd drugged her co-workers with the same shit they were pumping into the shifters to keep us calm. She'd unlocked all the cages, and disabled the alarms so the other test subjects could get out. There was a silverback in there they called Beast, and there is a hundred percent chance he killed every one of those lab workers before he left. He'd been in there the longest. He was even more fucked up than me. I don't know if Alice knew, but she'd probably granted him vengeance he'd been planning since the day they'd taken him from his family group and brought him in." Clinton cracked his knuckles loudly. "After I got out, I tracked down my parents. They'd moved to a new state to distance themselves from the fallout, and nothing was familiar. Not even me. I got tired of seeing the worry in their eyes—like their baby had been switched at birth and they didn't know if they could love the one they had. So I found a crew of bachelor bears. Fucked that up, moved to another, and another. Ended up in Damon's mountains, back near my hometown, because I heard an alpha was willing to take problem bears and was trying not to put them down."

"Put them down?"

"We police our own. Crazy shifters are killed by an alpha. I knew if I was lucky, Creed would let me go out with honor, but he was too damned patient. Believed in me, or some hippy dippy shit. The Gray Backs started pairing up, and I was pissed because I'd finally found a place I felt okay, and they were ruining it. They were drawing too much attention, breeding. Our population was exploding, and I could see it coming." He dragged sad eyes to her. "I just had this feeling that we would burn, but this time it would be the end of everything because it wasn't just a bunch of bachelors. It would be their mates and kids. Their families. It would be me losing more people I…"

"Love."

Clinton winced and shook his head. "I don't use that word."

"Why not?"

He kissed her wrist again and pulled back onto the main road. "Because nothing hurts worse than love."

****

She'd wanted to argue with him. She'd wanted to tell Clinton that rejection hurt, but that love was the greatest feeling in the world. But the more she thought about it, the more she considered the possibility that perhaps love really had poisoned him. He had an animal side that had been manipulated to bond to a woman who abused him. And that's what he'd known of love. It wasn't real love by any normal standards, but to Clinton, that's what he knew of it. If she had been hurt sexually and emotionally over and over and over by someone calling what they were doing "love," then perhaps she would hate the idea of it, too.

But a tiny, selfish part of her was saddened by the thought that she might very well never hear those three coveted words from his lips.

Alyssa hated Amber with the heat of a trillion meteors. A surprising, beastly corner of her heart was glad Clinton had given her a bear and killed her. Amber deserved to die at the hands of the boy she had destroyed.

Boarland Mobile Park read the sign over the white gravel road. As her gaze landed on the largest singlewide trailer facing them, she couldn't help but smile at the strange sensation that came over her. That must be 1010. It was cute that Bash thought it had magic, and even cuter that Clinton wanted her to stay there for undisclosed reasons. Perhaps he believed in magic, too.

Clinton's leg bounced in quick succession, as if he was nervous, so she rested her hand on his powerful thigh and gave him an encouraging smile. "I've already met the Boarlanders. I like them."

"Yeah," he said noncommittally. "Everything will be okay." It sounded like he was trying to convince himself more than her, though.

Clinton drove to the back of the park to a small trailer sitting catty-corner to 1010. The words *FUCK THE NEW RULES* had been burned neatly into the weedy yard. Stunned, she got out and made her way to the scorch marks.

"Don't judge." Clinton's voice was soft, pleading.

"I'm actually really impressed with how perfect this looks. Is the font Times New Roman?"

Clinton looked uncertain and suspicious all at once. "Yes."

"How did you perfectly burn an actual font into the yard?"

"Thank you!" He held his hands out and yelled it louder. "Thank you! Finally, someone sees the effort in my artwork. I spent an entire week pissing on Harrison's front lawn last month. An *entire week*, every piss, just so I could kill his grass into the perfect shape of a penis, and not a single one of these assholes complimented it." Clinton sauntered toward the beat-up old trailer and muttered, "They all just bitched about me acting out again."

Alyssa laughed hard, and damn it felt good after the emotional roller coaster of a morning they'd had. She could just imagine him out there in the middle of the night drawing a cartoon penis on his alpha's sod. It was new enough still to show the squares of grass in perfect lines in front of each trailer. Except for Clinton's. Apparently he'd refused to conform. She giggled again. *That's my man.*

Clinton's trailer was a patch-work wreck. A third of it had been destroyed at some point, but it had been repaired, and that part spray-painted in camouflage shades of green. The front door, which looked new and had been stained a rich, chestnut brown, boasted the neatly written words, *Fuck off*, in red spray paint.

The other trailers in the park were white, with matching porches and new roofs and lush landscaping, but Clinton's was a disaster. Bright side—at least she would never mistake which was his.

"So you know," Clinton muttered, his hand resting on the doorknob, "no woman has ever been in my house."

"Good. I like that I'm your first lady visitor."

He hesitated another few seconds, then pushed the door open. And as Alyssa stepped inside, she was shocked to her marrow at what she found. She'd expected the bachelor pad to look like a tornado had hit it, but he'd turned the place into a mountain cabin on the inside, complete with log walls, exposed rafters, and furniture in burgundy and green moose and bear patterns. The living space was small, but open to the kitchen to give a feeling of openness. And the kitchen itself was incredible. She ran her finger along the brown, black, and gold swirls of the polished granite countertops. It even had a massive dark bronze farm sink, and a set of earth-toned hand-thrown dishes sat in a drying rack on the counter.

When she turned back to Clinton, her face must've been frozen into a mask of shock because he crossed his arms over his chest and shifted his weight to the side, the picture of discomfort. "Everyone else was making nice houses, and Bash gave me a budget. I don't give a shit about the outside, but this space is for me."

"Clinton," she huffed on a breath. "I *love* your home."

A quick glance at her, and then there was that slight smile again. "It's pretty fuckin' awesome, right?"

"Really awesome! Look!" She jammed her finger across the living room. "You have a hammock! Inside!"

She was stunned when Clinton flashed a bigger smile. Straight white teeth peeked out from behind his beard, and his grin crinkled his dancing eyes slightly in the corners. Clinton was the most beautiful man she'd ever seen.

"You want to lay in it?"

Alyssa stripped out of her jacket and hung it on the coat rack, then made her way across the refurbished wood floors to the hammock. With one last excited glance at her man, she settled into it carefully. "Now feed me grapes and fan me."

Clinton snorted. "I can feed you beer and tacos and open the window."

She snickered. "Good enough."

"Clinton!" someone yelled from outside.

"What?" he screamed.

"Do you want to go camping tonight?"

Clinton growled and threw open the door. "Why the fuck would we go camping, Harrison? We live in a trailer park. We're basically camping right now."

"Okay, I was trying to be nice and ask you politely, but since you're being your usual asshole self, we're all going camping as a crew. Pack up."

"Hard pass."

"Clinton, pack your shit up and let's go. You have an hour."

Clinton roared at his alpha so hard his veins popped out of his neck, then he slammed the door.

For a moment, there was nothing but the noise of the creaking hammock, but then he turned to her, looking cool as a cucumber. "You want to go camping?"

"Uhh, I thought you didn't want to go."

"Nah, that's just a show for Harrison. Everyone gets worried if I get to pliable. I love camping."

Alyssa burst out laughing. "You are the terror of the trailer park, aren't you?"

"Do you find that sexy?"

"Extremely."

He strode over to the fridge and threw it open. "Then yes. Do you drink real beer or that girly fruity shit beer? I have the regular stuff in stock, but I'll have to ask Bash if he has any of the girly ones. He probably still has those stupid little miniature umbrellas to put in them. Or I know for a fact he has, like, eight boxes of wine."

"I don't really like any beer or wine. I don't like the taste of alcohol."

Clinton tossed her a frown over his shoulder like he didn't understand that word combination. "What do you drink when you go to bars?"

"Whatever gets me drunk quick so I can't taste the alcohol anymore."

Clinton's grin turned wicked. "You ever had trashcan punch?"

"Sounds disgusting."

"It is for about one sip, and then you don't taste nothin'. We're gonna trailer park it up tonight then. Come on. I have to get Big Blue."

"What's that?" she asked, flopping ungracefully from the hammock onto the floor.

Clinton was rummaging through a cabinet above the stove, pulling down bottles of liquor. "Big Blue is a cooler."

"I didn't bring any extra clothes for camping," Alyssa murmured, looking down at her dark wash skinny jeans and flip-flops.

"You're dressed fine. We probably won't sleep anyway. Just wear that. I'll bring you one of my sweaters and a blanket, too, just in case you get cold. And then if you're still cold, you can give me a hand-job in the sleeping bag and warm yourself up." He waggled his eyebrows once and went back to shoving the alcohol he'd collected into a cardboard box.

Damn, after what he'd been through, she was proud that he could joke about that stuff with her.

"Come on, woman. You're helping make the camp booze."

"I'm a terrible bartender."

"And I'm a shit teacher, but you can't really screw up trashcan punch."

Okay then. Alyssa snatched her jacket off the rack as Clinton tugged her out the front door, the box of libations tucked under his other arm.

The trailer park had been quiet a few minutes ago when they'd driven in, but now it was organized chaos as everyone was running around excitedly, packing supplies into the back of a giant red pickup with black rims and rooster tails of mud splattered down both sides.

But when they saw Alyssa, one by one, the Boarlanders slowed their action and gathered behind the red truck.

Clinton shoved his way through them and set the box on the tailgate. Then he yanked a giant blue cooler from the back and tossed the bystanders a filthy look. "What?"

"Hi, Alyssa!" Bash said.

"Oh." Clinton slung his arm over her

shoulders and lifted his chin. "This is mine. Don't touch, or I'll eat you."

"She is your what?" Harrison asked carefully, his blue eyes sparking with challenge.

Clinton shrugged. "Just...mine. And I don't want to hear shit about it either, so save it."

"Holy crap," Kirk said around a red rope candy that hung from his mouth. The behemoth was looking at Alyssa as if he'd never seen her before.

"I like your red toenails," Bash said.

"Thank you." Alyssa grinned and held her foot out, spreading her toes. "Clinton painted them."

The red rope candy hit the dirt, and now Kirk was staring at Clinton with his mouth hanging open. The others all wore similar expressions.

"Your faces all look so dumb right now," Clinton said through a smirk. "I'm gonna be better at this than all y'all." He sauntered off toward one of the other trailers. "The bar has been raised, dirtbags." He twirled his hand in the air and flipped them off over his shoulder.

Alyssa was trying not to laugh, really she was, but Clinton was hilarious. It would've been different if he really meant offense, but this was the show to distance himself from people. And what a show it was, because she'd seen the real, quiet, gritty side of him. She loved both.

Beck recovered first. "Hi," she drawled out, her light green eyes wide as she offered her hand. "I know we all met at Moosey's, but I guess I just didn't think we would ever see you again because Clinton is…well…Clinton." She shook Alyssa's hand hard enough to rattle her bones, and then introduced everyone officially, even little Air-Ryder, who was drawing on the porch of one of the trailers with colorful sidewalk chalk.

Harrison's gaze was still locked on where Clinton had disappeared into a trailer near the front of the park. "Uh, Alyssa? I'd like to extend a formal invitation to join us on our camping trip tonight."

"I sure appreciate it, and I whole-heartedly accept. I haven't been camping in forever. I'm not really wearing the right shoes, but Clinton said that was okay."

"What size are you?" Audrey asked.

"Seven and a half."

The alpha's mate nodded and offered Alyssa a pure and genuine smile. "I've got you covered. Come on, girlie."

She tugged Alyssa's hand toward the first trailer on the left of the Boarland Mobile Park sign. And thirty minutes later, Audrey had Alyssa all decked out in calf high hiking boots lined in faux fur over her skinny jeans, and an extra sweater that hugged her curves. She thought she looked pretty good in her new get-up, and when she stepped outside, chatting excitedly with Audrey, Emerson, and Ally, Clinton's hungry attention said she looked all right by him, too. He dragged that sexy silver gaze up and down her body twice as she approached, lingering on her curves. With a grin, she pulled her folded jacket away from her and did a slow spin.

"Woman, you look fine as hell," Clinton said as he unscrewed the lid of a bottle of Everclear.

"Wait, are we doing trashcan punch tonight?" Ally asked, a hint of excitement in her voice.

"Sure are," Clinton muttered as he poured an entire bottle of Everclear and one of tequila into Big Blue.

"What can I do to help?" Alyssa asked.

"Slice up those oranges and toss 'em in, sexy."

She and the girls settled into a line against

the tailgate, cutting up fruit and cracking up as they tossed the sliced citrus into the cooler with the liquor. Audrey poured in a giant jug of fruit punch, and Ally dumped in frozen cans of pineapple juice and limeade, and when they were done and the cooler was half-full, Alyssa ripped the top of a giant bag of ice and poured it in carefully.

And then when they'd stacked the back of Harrison's truck and Clinton's truck with boxed tents and roll-up sleeping bags, food, charcoal, a small mountain of snacks, bottled waters, juice boxes for Air-Ryder, and a hoard of those multi-colored, fabric bag-chairs, they piled into the trucks and were off.

As Alyssa bounced side to side with the ruts of the washed-out back roads up into the mountains beside her man, she couldn't stop smiling. Today was definitely not like any day she'd ever had in her life. Everyone was being so nice, and welcoming, and she loved watching the different dynamics in the Boarlander crew. Everyone joked and teased, but no one got offended or hurt. Instead, there was this beautiful ebb and flow of laughter and banter.

Clinton flashed her one of those good smiles as he navigated the muddy road behind

Harrison's truck, and then shocked her to stillness when he leaned over and kissed her on the lips quick. Just a peck to say he cared about her, and he didn't mind who was in the back seat watching them.

She felt completely and publically claimed in front of the people Clinton cared about the most, and it meant more to her than she could ever express.

Today had been the most emotional day in her memory.

But it had also been the best.

TWELVE

What was this strange feeling in his chest? This annoying flapping that happened when Shae laughed or came back with a witty retort to one of the Boarlanders' teasing.

They were giving her a hard time for choosing him, but it meant they were accepting her. If they ignored her, or gave her the cold shoulder, then Clinton would've been nervous. As it stood, Shae was like a damn snake-charmer, Boarlander edition.

He fuckin' loved watching her slip into this notch that had been missing from the crew. He'd picked well. Good bear. At least the monster was good for something. Shae. She was the best part of him. The brightest.

Her giggle trailing off, she took another sip of trashcan punch from her red plastic cup and snuggled against his side. In a rush, she tensed and retreated, but he grabbed her arm and prevented her escape. She'd been doing that—forgetting to be careful.

"I'm okay," he murmured against her ear. "I like you up against me."

He and the boys had dragged up logs around the fire they'd made, and they were all leaning against them, relaxed, plates of half-eaten food in laps, cups all around, smiles on every face. Hell, maybe he was even smiling. He'd never given a single thought to what his face was doing until Shae had told him his smile "felt like home." Home? Yeah, made sense to him. They had been each other's everything when they were kids. Some part of her had clung to that. God, he was so lucky that she'd come back to him.

Clinton picked up his drink and looked inside. It was full, an orange slice floating at the top. Shockingly, he was sober. Why? Because Shae was doing something strange to him. She was making him want to be clearheaded in case she needed anything, in case she needed his protection, in case she didn't like Drunk Clinton.

Shae swatted a bug off Emerson's leg and said, "I just saved your life."

"My hero," Emerson swooned. "Oh!"

Emerson grabbed Shae's hand and pressed it against her belly. Clinton could see the languid movement of her baby from here, and he couldn't help but smile when Shae lowered her lips to Emerson's belly and said, "Halloooo, baby bear cub."

Bash chimed in. "I'm gonna put, like, thirty babies in her."

"That is untrue," Emerson said. "He'll put maybe two, and then this baby-factory is closed. Being pregnant is hard."

Across the fire, Beck snuggled closer to Mason, who cuddled a sleeping Air-Ryder against his chest. And the smile they gave each other was so tender, Clinton had to look away.

Someday, he would give a baby to Shae if she wanted to build a family with him. Far from now, when he was better and more stable. He would never admit it out loud, but he'd been watching Mason, taking notes, because someday he hoped to be the type of father he was to Air-Ryder.

He'd never dreamed of that until Shae had come back into his life. He was a broken vase, shattered on the floor, and she was his glue. She made him think about what he wanted. Made him think about goals and improvement since he wouldn't be able to keep her like he was.

Shae pulled her cell phone from her pocket and frowned at the screen.

"Who is it?" he asked. Nosy? Probably, but he liked to know everything about her.

"My parents." Shae shrugged. "They have been calling a lot, which means they found out I came here, but I don't want the lectures."

"What lectures?"

"They raised me in a bubble. Small town, and while I was recovering, they had a tendency to alienate me. My old friends never came around, and my parents got paranoid every time I tried to take a risk. And I love them, so eventually, I just stopped worrying them by becoming the most boring creature on the face of the planet. They'll tell me to come back home if I open up a line of communication."

"You should answer. They worry. You're a grown-ass woman on vacation. They can't keep you from that stuff, but you can let them know you're safe."

Shae snorted. "My parents would love you."

Clinton allowed a dark chuckle. "I don't know about that." They had loved him once, but then everything had gone to hell.

Shae pouted up at him, her eyes so big and beautiful, her cheeks glowing with the pulsing light of the fire. Unable to help himself, he dipped his lips to hers and sucked that pout gently from her bottom lip. He loved the way she melted against him in an instant, like they were meant to be one person. Good mate, always reacting to him and making it easy to lose himself in touching her. He'd been afraid Amber's damage would reach its inky tendrils from his hardened heart right into Shae's, but so far, it had been the easiest thing in the world to trust his mate with his body.

When he eased away—mostly because he was now rocking one enormous boner—she let off a happy little noise and smiled drunkenly at him, her eyelids heavy. "I'm going to call my mom real quick."

Clinton bit her neck gently until she giggled and eased back. "I'll keep your spot warm. Good luck."

And a few minutes later, she returned with a slight frown marring her pretty face. As she settled back beside him, she said, "Huh. They told me they loved me and were proud of me, and that they hoped I had fun for the rest of my trip."

"That's good." Phew, because he had been

a little worried Dana would let it slip about Shae's past.

"And then they said they were really sorry, but when I asked what for, they clammed up and said their goodbyes." Her dark eyebrows arched high. "That was weird, right?"

"You're asking Crazy Clinton if something is weird?" Kirk slurred. "He's not going to be your best gauge of normalcy."

Ally had her legs draped across her mate's legs and was cuddled against his side, but at Kirk's insult she said, "Hey now. I've literally never seen Clinton so un-crazy as he has been tonight. Alyssa is magic. She is Clinton's ten-ten."

"I'm gonna check the border of the campsite," Harrison announced, standing. "Clinton, why don't you come?"

"No, thank you. Go take a piss by yourself, alpha. Girls go to the bathroom in herds. I ain't a woman, and you don't need protection from the bogeyman."

Harrison's lips thinned into a pissed-off line, and Clinton already knew what was coming next—the order. "Now, Clinton."

The power of his words wafted across Clinton's skin and cowed his animal. Damn it all, he hated when Harrison pulled this crap.

Clinton didn't hold back the snarl in his chest, but he kicked out of the blanket and stood. "Fine. I'll be right back," he told Shae, then followed Harrison out into the dark woods.

"Look, if you want someone to hold your dick for you, you should know I don't touch anything in miniature—"

"Who is she?" Harrison asked low.

Clinton crossed his arms over his chest and pled the fifth.

"I talked to your first alpha, and you know what he told me?"

"Carl is a vagina who should shut the hell up about other peoples' personal business."

"He said you had a mate named Shalene Dunleavy, who died, and another mate, who also died. So imagine my surprise when a girl with the same last name as your first mate shows up, and your bear is already so deep in devotion to her, that you, the biggest, single pain in my ass, grows manners overnight. Who. The fuck. Is she?"

Clinton tossed a glance through the woods to the soft glow of the fire some distance away. "She's my first mate. My only maybe, I don't know."

"So she didn't die?"

"No, and I didn't tell Carl she died. I told

him I lost her, which I did. And she might as well have died because she has no memory of her old life or of me. Happy?"

"You should tell her who you are."

"Fuck off, Harrison." He made to leave, but Harrison gripped his arm and prevented it.

Clinton growled a warning. "Careful, alpha. This story is much deeper than you can guess."

"Then enlighten me. You lying to her? She'll find out, and when she does, you'll lose her."

"And if I tell her, I'll lose her."

The fire left Harrison's eyes, and uncertainty flashed across his face.

He released Clinton like a good bear, so he tossed him a bone. "Shae was taken from me and from her family when she was sixteen. For two years, she was in a testing facility because they thought she was me. They thought she was a bear shifter. They probably found out real quick she couldn't Change, but they needed humans for their program, too. It was two fuckin' years before I could find her and negotiate her release."

"With what?"

"With myself. And part of the deal was that her memories were wiped. That's the only way they were gonna let her live after what she'd seen, and I was okay with that."

"Shhhhit." Harrison linked his hands behind his head and took two steps back. Smart man because Clinton's bear was ripping at his insides to bleed that mother fucker.

"If you were me, and Audrey had been taken, and if God-knows-what had been done to her in that two years, would you force her to relive that? Or would you let her move on and just go hard trying to make her happy for the rest of her life?"

Harrison's eyes were on the fire in the distance for a long time before he murmured, "I don't know, man."

Clinton lowered his voice to an angry whisper. "I just got her back. I just got a second chance. I'm trying not to fuck it up, so please keep this shit to yourself and let me keep her."

Harrison looked sick, but he nodded and murmured, "Okay. I won't say anything."

Clinton cracked his knuckles. With a pissed-off sigh that tapered into a growl, he strode off. And because he was working on himself for Shae's sake, he remembered his manners and muttered, "Thank you," over his shoulder.

There was no right or wrong answer.

Telling her what had happened would get her scratching at memories that needed to stay buried. What would it help if she remembered what had happened to her? She would be as dark as him. Two years had ruined him. Poisoned him. Killed the good parts of him, and he wanted better for Shae.

He wanted her to be happy.

Clinton was willing to lie to her until her dying breath to keep her safe from the awful memories she'd made between those white walls. Screw what that said about him. The truth was for do-gooders, but he didn't give a shit about anything other than Shae's smiles.

He wasn't lying to her.

He was protecting her.

THIRTEEN

Alyssa startled awake, every muscle tensed. It was dark and smelled of earth and pine sap.

Where was she?

A strange, familiar sensation washed through her, and she bolted upright.

Something heavy fell from her waist to her lap. "What's wrong?" Clinton asked, his arm tightening around her hips.

Right. She was in a tent, not somewhere scary. She was camping with Clinton, and he would never, ever let anything bad happen to her. He was big, protective, and even if he hadn't said it, even if he never would, he loved her.

When her eyes began to adjust to the darkness, she became better anchored in the here and now.

"Did you have a dream?" Clinton asked low.

Jerkily, she nodded her head and drew her knees up to her chest. "Yes. Just a dream." The air outside of their blankets was cold, and she was only wearing one of Clinton's oversize thermal sweaters.

"*The* dream?" he asked.

"No. This was something different."

Clinton's massive form relaxed back onto the pallet he'd made late last night. He'd set up their tent ridiculously far away from the others, but he said that his bear needed distance, especially with his protective instincts kicked up right now. "I had four brothers," Clinton murmured. His eyes were silver and glowing strangely as he looked at her and stroked her hair. "We all slept in the same room, and my youngest brother, Tim, had night terrors somethin' fierce. And my mom, she never got irritated at being woke up in the middle of the night. Not like me and my other brothers. She would sit on the edge of his bed—he was on the bottom bunk under me—and she would say, 'Tim, always tell someone your bad dreams, and it'll take the power from them. They won't ever come true if you share them with someone.'"

Slowly, Alyssa settled under the blankets and against Clinton's side. She rested her cheek against his chest as he tightened his strong arm around her.

"You won't like it."

Clinton made a single ticking sound behind his teeth and cut off a soft snarl in his throat. "I fucked up with that. I should've listened to your dream and not made you keep it. I won't do that anymore." He swallowed audibly in the dark. "Tell me."

"I wasn't me," she whispered. "I was some other girl. Shae. And the boy was there. And he was so…"

"Say it."

"He was so handsome, smiling all the time as we walked through these woods. Evergreens and blackberry bushes. It smelled like here. The sun was so bright, and it would blind me sometimes. I was seeing flashes. The boy looking behind him as we walked this dirt road. Our hands linked as he led me, always talking. Always smiling. And his eyes…he cared for me. For Shae." A tear streaked down the corner of her eye and pooled on his chest. "I was happy. I mean…that no-problems-in-the-whole-world kind of happy. I was barefoot, and I stepped on something sharp.

When the boy bent down to check it out, my toenails were painted red, and it matched the bleeding cut right on the side of my big toe. The boy told me it would be okay, it wasn't deep, and he would carry me back. When he looked up at me, his eyes were lighter, more white than silver, and the smile had gone from his face. We turned to walk back down that dirt road, but the boy froze. Just…turned into a statue. 'Let's go this way,' he said, and then picked me up like I weighed nothing and carried me off the road and into the woods. And I could see it then. It was a black car. A Jeep or Range Rover, I don't know."

Clinton pulled her closer to his side, his heartbeat banging against her cheek fast.

"Do you want me to stop?"

"No. Finish it." His voice sounded too low, too gravelly, but he'd said it would never come true if she told him, so she did.

"Four men got out, and the boy ran. And ran and ran, and I was so scared because I could hear them behind us. They were loud in the woods, not like the boy. He was quiet. He hid me under a fallen log that had rotted in the middle, told me he would draw them away, and I waited there, frozen, the sound of my heartbeat deafening. It was so loud I thought they would hear it and find me. I was so scared, listening for those awful people. There was shouting far away, and I just knew they'd caught the boy, so I lurched up out of the log and bolted for the sound. I had to save him. He felt like everything. And then someone grabbed me from behind, and I sucked in this deep breath to scream… And then I woke up here." Alyssa closed her eyes tightly to rid herself of the moisture that rimmed them.

"Why didn't you stay put?" Clinton rasped out.

"I didn't have control," she squeaked out. "I wasn't me." It was just a dream. She couldn't be held responsible for actions during a dream!

Clinton gripped the back of her neck and kissed her hard. He didn't move his lips or push for more. He just sat there smashed against her, his lips hard and unforgiving. And then with a helpless sound, he thrust his tongue into her mouth. She knew what he was doing. He was taking that dream away from her and reminding her where she was. That awful dream wasn't real. This was. He was.

Alyssa slid her arms around his neck and held him close. This time, he didn't balk or panic at being trapped. He rolled his hips against hers instead, encouraging her. Clinton slept naked, and his erection was impossibly hard against her belly. Her sweater was pissing her off, keeping them apart. She needed to feel his warm skin against hers. Needed to feel the safety he brought. Clinton would never let anything bad happen to her, never ever. She knew it down to her bones that he would take care of her. She could trust him.

He would never leave her like the boy had left Shae.

She struggled to push the sweater up her stomach while mashed against his rock-hard torso, but Clinton had other ideas and just ripped the dang thing. Just…tore it down the middle like the thick sweater material was rice paper. Delicious chills trembled up her spine at his raw power. He kept it hidden, she knew, but little by little, he was letting her in. He was letting her see him.

He smelled of fur now, and she was so friggin' revved up she couldn't control her body. He pushed the sweater off her arms and held her so close her breasts ached. Too hard. Clinton was kissing too hard, which would've been great if he didn't have that damned beard. Alyssa bit his lip, then dipped her throbbing lips to his neck and trailed kisses to his chest. She nibbled gently on his pierced nipple until he arched against her and grunted a sexy, needy sound. God, she loved him like this. Every time she dared a look, his eyes were glowing and hungry, his teeth gritted, his face feral. Hers. This wild man was hers.

Clinton rolled her on top of him, but this was a lot and fast. Too fast? "Clinton, are you sure?"

"Amber ain't here. It's just you and me." He lowered his voice to a barely audible whisper. "Take me back."

Take him back how? Straddling him, she settled over his dick and rolled her hips. Clinton gripped her thighs hard, and she loved he was desperate for her right now. She slid over his shaft slowly. Clinton bowed his neck back, flexing his thick muscles as he rolled his eyes closed. In a blur, he sat up and kissed her, held her in place over his lap and rocked his hips to the rhythm she set. He felt so good here, chest against hers, holding her tight, touching her clit just right with every thrust. She wouldn't last long like this, not with the fire burning so bright in her middle. Not when every stroke filled her with glorious, tingling pressure. Not when his hard body felt this good against hers.

I love you. The words were on the tip of her tongue, but Clinton didn't like that word—love—so she wouldn't use it on him now. He wasn't there, and maybe he never would be, but instinct told her she could tell him in another way.

Oh, she knew the laws. Knew it was illegal for humans and shifters to mark each other, but she gave zero fucks as he pushed into her again, so deep. Clinton was hers, and for some strange reason, he felt like maybe he always had been. They'd been on colliding paths, two broken souls who belonged together.

So close. He felt so right buried so far inside of her, and now his arms were shaking, tensed. He was straining with every time he bucked into her, and she lowered her lips to his shoulder, the one without the tattoos because, if he allowed this, she wanted everyone to see her mark on him. She wanted Amber to see it from the fires of hell.

Testing, she opened her mouth and bit down on the hardened muscle there. Clinton's response was instant. His hand was on the back of her head in a moment, and the snarl that ripped through his chest was nothing short of beastly. He pressed her closer, encouraging her as he smoothed out his pace inside of her.

"Do it," he gritted out in a voice she didn't recognize.

My monster.

The first explosive pulse of orgasm tensed her body. So good. So right. Squeezing her eyes tightly closed, Alyssa bit into his skin as hard as she could. Until her jaw ached, until she tasted iron, until the air smelled of pennies and her mouth was filled with warmth. If it hurt him, Clinton didn't show it. He pulled her closer and went rigid as his dick throbbed hard inside of her. She released his torn skin and gasped, throwing her head back as he rocked inside of her, filling her with jet after hot jet of wetness.

His pace slowed as he dragged out every aftershock. His body twitched, and he hugged her tight and buried his face against her neck. He nipped her there, but nothing more, and she got it. Giving her a claiming mark would mean he would put a bear inside of her, and after killing Amber with one, something deep inside Alyssa said he wouldn't make the same offer to her, even if she wanted to be a shifter like him.

This would be enough. He had laid a

claiming mark on her heart. And maybe others wouldn't see it, but she and Clinton would always share this beautiful secret. They would always know it was there.

As she held him close in the dark, as she smelled his skin and absorbed the warm safety he emanated, she knew the mark she'd just given wasn't just some moment of passion.

Clinton had never been Amber's mate.

The Fates had decided long ago that he was always meant for Alyssa.

FOURTEEN

"Well, I'm really gonna miss you around here," Angie murmured, "but I'm really, really happy for you."

"I'm not!" Bryce called from the background. "I have to do everything around here now."

Alyssa laughed and shook her head. "I miss you guys, too, but I'll be back in a few weeks to pick up my things, and we'll go out and have some fun. And we'll talk on the phone all the time." Alyssa pulled into an open space in the giant field outside the park where the Lumberjack Wars had been set up. Her phone beeped, and quick as a blink, she checked the text message that flashed over her screen. It was Beck. *Where are you?!*

"Oh, Angie, I have to get going. I'm working an event today, and it's a big one to get more votes."

"Two weeks out. Are you nervous?"

"Oh, my gosh, so nervous! I never thought a vote would affect me so much, but Clinton and I can't move forward at all if the shifters don't get their rights back. Not legally. We'll be stuck where we are for always."

"Well, Bryce and I are rallying here, girl. If you need anything, you just let us know."

"I will. And Angie?"

"Yeah?"

"Thanks. I mean it. For everything. For encouraging me to come after Clinton, for doing that fundraiser for me to take a vacation here, for setting up this trip, for giving me a job all those years and being such an awesome boss. I owe you so much."

"No need for thanks. I'm happy to be a part of your story, Alyssa. It's an incredible one. I'm glad Clinton turned out to be the perfect match for you."

Butterflies flapped around Alyssa's middle, and she beamed. "Me, too. I'm happy here." Her phone beeped again. "Oh, Angie, I really have to go. I'll call you tonight. Tell Bryce hi and I miss him!"

Bryce called in the background, "Miss you, too! Don't forget to shave your legs!"

Angie laughed and said her goodbye.

Alyssa hung up and kicked open the door to her Sunfire, then bolted for the trunk. She had four boxes of calendars for the autograph booth, but there was no way her scrawny arms would carry them all at once. She would have to make a couple of trips.

"Let me help," a giant of a man said from right beside her.

She startled hard and clutched her chest, and Creed, the dark-haired grizzly shifter alpha of the Gray Backs apologized through a lopsided grin. "Beck asked me to wait out front to help you bring this stuff in. Thanks for going back for the extra boxes, by the way. The boys are blowing through the stock Beck brought."

Over the past few days, she'd met most of the shifters in Damon's mountains, but she hadn't ever talked to Creed in person. She arched her neck way back to look him in the eyes when she thanked him. Wow, he was intimidating.

He stacked three boxes in his arms and pointed his chin at her yellow Team Clinton T-shirt. "Nice. I think you're the only one he gave one to, but be warned, Beck is selling stacks of them right now for the charity. Clinton's pissed. Says he only wants you wearing one.

God, he's a beast today. Beck will be glad you're here to help manage him."

Alyssa grabbed the last box and shut the trunk, then asked, "Why? What's he doing?"

"Well, it's the Boarlanders' shift to sign calendars between their events, and Clinton signed the first twenty or so *don't masturbate to me* right across his picture. He ruined lots of Januarys before Beck ripped into him, and now he's just drawing pictures of huge penises on his photograph. I mean, long, flopped out on the ground, smiley-faced dicks everywhere."

Alyssa cracked up and shook her head. She should be horrified, but that was just Clinton, and likely, his attitude wasn't going anywhere.

She'd had to park in the back so she maneuvered through a tight place between cars. Probably eight more rows, and they would reach the entrance.

"So," Creed drawled, looking a little sheepish. "I kind of lied. Beck didn't send me so much as I volunteered so I could get a minute with you before the chaos of today."

"Why? What do you need?"

"No, no. Well…first off, I really appreciate all the help you've been giving Beck lately with our public relations. With her being newly pregnant and everything, it was a big strain being the publicist for all of us, and I know it's made a big difference her bein' able to depend on you. We all really appreciate it. But I also wanted to thank you for whatever you're doing for Clinton."

Alyssa slowed, utterly baffled. "What do you mean?"

Creed licked his bottom lip and twitched his head to the side. "Clinton came to Grayland Mobile Park yesterday morning. And that might not seem like a big deal, but he left us badly. Just ran, and we were pissed and hurt that he'd gone to the Boarlanders. He hasn't visited the park since he left. But yesterday he came and called a meeting, and…" Creed shook his head and jacked up his dark eyebrows under his baseball cap. "Well, Clinton apologized and said he was real happy for all of us and the mates we've found. He said he was proud of us."

Alyssa pursed her lips against her emotions. That was a really big deal for Clinton to own his time with the Gray Backs and to come clean with the guilt he carried leaving like he did. She'd known he had wanted to make amends, but hearing about it from Creed was different. It meant so much that the Gray Backs appreciated the monumental effort it took Clinton to build up to going back there.

"Anyway, I know you have something to do with him being okay now." Creed bumped her shoulder gently and lowered his voice. "Whatever you're doing, you're saving him, and that means the world to me. If you ever need anything, you come to me. I owe you."

Alyssa smiled emotionally up at him. "He's the one saving me," she squeaked out past her tightening vocal cords.

Creed chuckled and waited for her to pass another tight spot between cars before he followed. "And also, it's pretty badass what you did."

"What did I do?"

"Clinton has shown everyone in Damon's mountains that scar on his shoulder. Looks a helluva lot like a claiming mark to me."

"Oh God, he's going to get me arrested."

"Alyssa, the criminal."

"Quit it," she muttered.

Creed nodded to the lady at the ticket booth. "She's a Boarlander."

And now the butterflies were back. She'd never been called a Boarlander before, but damn, it felt good.

The attendant offered Alyssa a genuine smile, handed her a free drink ticket, and waved her on through without collecting her fifteen dollars.

"Thank you!" Alyssa told her, adjusting the box in her arms. "Wow," she said to Creed as they made their way down a long, crowded row of food vendors in colorful tents. "I feel VIP."

He snorted. "Yeah, you can't marry the man you love, your mark on him is illegal as hell, and you can't officially register to your crew, but you get into the Lumberjack Wars for free. You're so lucky."

"Ha! Stop it. I am lucky." The luckiest, actually. And if this vote passed, she would be able to do all those things with Clinton someday.

She could tell where the shifters were signing their sexy calendars from all the news cameras. Harrison was standing with a reporter, looking laid back with an easy smile on his face as he talked with her. Beck The Miracle Worker had been training them all in the art of charming the masses, and at this point, all the Boarlanders were comfortable in front of news cameras except for Clinton, highlighted by the fact that, at the moment, he was pelvic thrusting in the background of Harrison's interview.

She followed Creed through the thick lines that led to the long table where Bash, Kirk, and Damon were sitting. They wore big grins, like they were actually enjoying themselves as they talked with people and signed their pictures on the calendars Beck had organized a couple months ago.

Alyssa had already bought one and had it pinned on the wall of 1010. Clinton was fine as hell, standing in front of his truck, smoke billowing from the chainsaw he held up in the air, his chin lifted, eyes fierce, abs ridiculously sexy, and his holey jeans riding low, giving just a peek at that trail of blond hair that led under his pants. All the months were super sexy, but Mr. January was her favorite by a lot.

"Clinton," she said at normal volume. She was used to his sensitive hearing now.

He stopped pelvic thrusting and jerked his wild, silver gaze to her. An instant smile took his face, a big one. She lived for those.

She set the box on the table near Beck and turned in time to catch him as he barreled down on her. He picked her up off the ground and nuzzled her neck until it tickled and she laughed and swatted his shoulder. "I heard you've been a little terror."

"Please. I've been good all morning."

"Disagree," Beck said through a narrow-eyed glare for Clinton. Her red-gold curls bounced as she swung her attention to Alyssa. "I'm really glad you're here. He behaves better with you around, and I swear to God Clinton, if you stick that middle finger up at me again, I'm gonna claw it off." Indeed, Beck's eyes were bright gold. Her snowy owl was likely good and done with wrangling Clinton today.

"I have a surprise for you," she told Clinton as he settled her on her feet.

"Is it a blow job?" He began frantically looking around at the surrounding tents like he was searching for a private hidey hole for them.

"No! Look." Alyssa lifted the hem of her jeans and showed him the brand new pair of knee-high yellow gym socks she'd put on this morning. "For luck."

Clinton spread his arms wide and took a few steps back, nodding his head like she was the sexiest thing he'd ever seen. Slowly, he bent and lifted the leg of his jeans and, sure enough, he had his favorite pair of socks on, too. Alyssa threw her arms around her stomach with her laughter.

"Clinton!" Beck barked out. She held a clipboard and jammed her pen at the chair on the end.

Indeed, the line on that one was backed up and ridiculously long, and people looked impatient.

"I have more surprises, but you have to put in your shift here and stop drawing penises on these nice peoples' calendars."

Clinton snarled up his lip and muttered, "Fine."

"One," she said, following him to his seat, "I'm down for a BJ tonight if you make Beck's job easy today. She's been fighting morning sickness, and she's stressed. You really will get clawed if you don't stop pestering her."

"BJ, yes." Clinton nodded and signed a calendar for a woman totally excited, bouncing on her toes as she waited. Was that seriously all he'd heard?

"Two, I quit my job at the diner back home today."

Clinton jerked his attention over his shoulder at her, his blond brows raised high. "Really?"

"Yep, because I landed that management position at Moosey's," she blurted excitedly. "Angie put in a good word, and I got the call back from Joey Dorsey today! I nailed the interview."

"Babe!" Clinton whooped. "I fucking knew you nailed it." He turned to the crowd. "She nailed it!"

A few confused women in the line gave her a slow clap, and with a chuckle, Alyssa began to organize the lopsided stacks of calendars around Clinton's cluttered station. Beck handed her a metal box, so she started taking the money and making change for Bash and Clinton's lines. Beck's eyes were finally softening to her human green color.

Mason strode through the crowd, Air-Ryder on his shoulders licking a red snow cone and grinning. "Ask your momma," Mason told him.

"Ask me what?" Beck sounded instantly happier.

"There's a log throwing event just for kids, and Mason said I could do it if you said it was okay."

"Well, when is it?"

"In just a few minutes," Mason said. "They said shifter kids could participate. I already asked."

When Beck tossed Alyssa a pleading look, she laughed. "Go on, watch your boy. I'll handle things here until you get back."

Beck hugged her shoulders and upped her voice to an uncomfortable octave. "Thank you, thank you! I'll be back right after it's through, I swear."

From where he was signing calendars, Bash pointed in the general direction of Alyssa's tits. "I like your shirt!" He turned his torso and showed Alyssa his own yellow Team Clinton shirt, and she laughed. The rest of the boys were wearing their own team shirts or Boarlander Bears shirts, but Bash was apparently throwing his support in for his ninth best friend.

And when she looked back to Clinton, he was watching the curve of her lips with the softest expression in his eyes. Going all emotional, she hugged his shoulders and rested her cheek against the top of his hair for a moment before he began signing another autograph. Without looking at her, he murmured. "I like you a lot."

Alyssa lifted her shoulders to her ears and resisted the squeal in her throat. That was a huge admission for him. She knew what he meant, so she lowered her mouth to his ear and whispered, "I love you, too."

She waited for him to go rigid and back

away from her, but he didn't. Instead, his cheeks tinted in a blush. He smiled at her, kissed her softly, and murmured, "Good."

FIFTEEN

Clinton took his cell phone and keys out of his back pocket and settled them into Alyssa's outstretched hand. God, why was she this nervous?

"You've got this, babe," she said as Clinton removed his T-shirt. Apparently that was the rule Beck had negotiated for the All-Shifter events today. No shirts so the ladies could ogle, and so the news and photographers could catch those muscle-ripping shots of the shifters going to work.

Her claiming mark was fully healed and was hard to see at a distance, but still, it was scary having it on display. Clinton cupped her neck and kissed her deeply, dipped his tongue against hers, nipped her bottom lip, and disengaged. Eyes bright, he gave her one last here-we-go look and then made his way to his log with Mason. They were the only two Boarlanders in this event. Mason gripped Clinton's shoulder, placing his hand perfectly over her mark as he talked low to Clinton. God, they were massive men.

The sheer volume of women at today's Lumberjack Wars had been record-breaking, and the awed murmurs from the crowd around her were intimidating. These boys would always get attention from women for what they were. Their instincts to protect their mates and rear young, and their masculine, powerful bodies were partially to thank for that.

Alyssa had worn her contacts today since it was sunny. She pushed her sunglasses farther up her nose as she read the towering score board a few events over. The Ashe Crew, Gray Backs, and Boarlanders were neck and neck, but this event could win it for her crew. And dang, it would be so awesome for them not to be C-Team anymore.

"Come on, Clinton!" she cheered, clapping as he made his way up onto the plank of wood sticking out of the thick log.

It bounced smoothly under his weight, but he balanced on it easily. His eyes were on Mason, who was right beside him and talking to him low, his eyes blazing the bright blue of his boar people. Kellen and Drew of the Ashe Crew were in this event, Beaston and Matt were representing the Gray Backs, and Kong had been an all-day one-man wrecking crew for his small Lowlander family group. And wow, all their eyes were blazing inhumanly bright. The event workers ten feet below the shifters' planks tossed up axes, and the competitors caught them easily. Arms rippling, tatted up, snarly, demon-eyed shifters, and all the ladies around her were cooling themselves with fans Beck had been handing out that said *Vote* with Cora Keller's pro-shifter website listed at the bottom for more information.

She understood those wide-eyed tipsy looks from the crowd. The shifters swayed slightly as they found their balance on the boards and pulled their axes back over one shoulder, readying for the horn. Clinton had her ovaries in a mushroom cloud right now.

"Come on, baby," she murmured, rocking up on the balls of her feet with nerves.

She squeezed his phone, and it vibrated. Crap, she probably pushed a button. Alyssa turned it over as it vibrated again. Someone was calling, but when she saw the number, the crowd disappeared around her. The cheering dulled, and even the air horn blasting the start of the event sounded muted and far away.

Why was Mom calling Clinton?

Her hand shook more and more with every ring as she stared at her house number on the glowing screen. Why was it labeled *home*? He hadn't met her parents yet. Hadn't even talked to them on the phone since she had planned on Clinton meeting them in person in a few weeks when she officially moved her stuff from North Carolina to 1010. When the phone stopped ringing, the *chop, chop* of the event echoed hollowly around in her mind.

"Clinton! Clinton! Clinton!"

People were cheering her man. She should be, too. There would be a good explanation.

She jacked her gaze up to the logs being chopped where Clinton was already halfway through, his powerful body twisting with each blow he sunk deep into the wood. His ax gleamed in the sunlight as he brought it back and swung again, chips of wood exploding outward on impact.

His phone dinged, and now it had a voicemail icon.

In a daze, Alyssa poked it and lifted his phone to her ear. Mom's recording came over the line, loud and clear. "Hi, Clinton. I was just calling to touch base. We haven't talked about what we're going to tell Alyssa in a few days. Craig and I are worried about that dream you told us about. It sounds like a memory, and if she's getting them back, we were thinking of coming clean. I know she's happy with you, though, so we wanted to include you in the decision. All right, we love ya, boy. Let us know what you're thinking. Bye."

Someone jostled her hard, and when she lowered the phone, Audrey and Beck were screaming and jumping, cheering loudly. "Clinton won! The Boarlanders won!"

The Boarlanders won. No more C-Team. More jostling, but everything felt so surreal. And when she looked up at Clinton's grinning face as he knocked axes with Mason on the log next to him, she just couldn't understand how he had this rapport with her parents. *We love ya, boy.* He'd told them about her dream, and mom said it was a memory? Her with the boy. Her being grabbed. That was a memory?

No. She backed up a few steps and ran into a barrel-chested man with his beer mug raised in the air. "Sorry," she murmured.

Clinton's eyes locked onto hers, and time slowed. His bright smile faded from his face, and his eyebrows lowered in confusion. He hopped off his plank, but she wanted to run. Run away from whatever betrayal he and her parents had cooked up. Run away from the hurt. Run away from him.

"What's wrong?" How had he gotten to her so fast? His eyes were light, more white than gray. *More white than gray*. Just like the boy in her dreams. She wanted to retch.

Alyssa wrenched her arm out of his grasp. "Why don't you ever say my name?"

"What?" he asked, matching her stride as she made her way past the outskirts of the crowd.

"I've thought about it, and I've never heard you say my name." She rounded on him. "Say it. Say Alyssa."

The fire cooled from Clinton's eyes, and he straightened up. His lips twisted into a stubborn line, and he gave his gaze to the tents nearby. Alyssa pushed him hard in the chest, but he didn't move. "Say it!"

He looked furious now as he blinked slowly and brought those blazing eyes to hers, his face angled to the side in warning.

Why was she crying? He didn't deserve to see her tears. "Say my name, Clinton. My real name."

His Adam's apple dipped into his throat.

"Shae."

"No." She shook her head and backed away, bit her bottom lip hard to punish the weak tremble there. "No."

She bolted for the front entrance, then sprinted past the gate and into the parking lot. Where was her damned car? Where had she parked? Frantically, she scanned the lot as she ran through row after row of cars. There it was, another five rows to go.

"Shae, stop," Clinton pleaded.

His hand on her arm was gentle enough, but she flinched away from him. "My fucking mom called." She held up his cell phone. "She left a voicemail about which way to spin your lies. You know me! You've known me all along. Tell me I'm wrong."

"If you'll just calm down, I'll tell you everything."

"Don't you fucking tell me to calm down!"

"Listen, I didn't tell you for a reason."

"What reason could you possibly have to lie to me? What reason, Clinton?"

He held his hands out like he was soothing a startled horse, but his eyes were blazing so bright they were hard to look at. The air felt heavy. Too heavy to breathe.

"I've known you all my life."

A sob wrenched from her throat. "Who am I?" she screamed.

Clinton looked gutted when he murmured, "Your name is Shalene Dunleavy. You were born here in Saratoga, and you lived a few doors down from the trailer I grew up in. Stop backing away." There was an edge to his voice. "Don't give me your back right now and don't run."

Chills blasted up her forearms. "You were the boy, Clinton. I guessed, and you told me you weren't."

"I'm not him anymore."

"I dreamed you traded yourself for Shae." She shook her head hard to rid herself of the creeping dizziness. "You traded yourself for me."

"I had to. You were there because of me. God, Shae, you should know you were there because of me, and whatever happened to you in there, you don't want to remember. You don't. You were taken when you were sixteen. I fought them. I couldn't fucking Change. My bear wouldn't work right when I was a kid, and I was trying so hard to just Change into my animal and kill those mother fuckers who were after us, but I couldn't. And when I woke up in the woods, I was bad off, and you weren't where I'd left you."

"The log." Her face fell, and tears streamed out of her eyes.

"They thought you were the bear shifter, and it took me two years of searching. Two years of you in that goddamned hell facility, and that was part of the deal. They would do a trade for me, but only if your memories were wiped. It was that or they would dispose of you." Clinton winced and shook his head hard. "And I agreed because that sounded like the perfect solution to me. I was going in, and I wouldn't get out, but I didn't want you remembering me or feeling guilty that I'd traded places with you. But more than anything, I didn't want you remembering whatever they did to you." Clinton shrugged. "I still don't! If I could've gotten away with this and your parents stayed on board, I would've taken this to my grave if it saved you from pain."

"And my parents were okay with lying to me, too? Alyssa isn't even my name!"

"It is. It is. The medicine they gave you worked for a long time. Months after you got out. You would lose a memory a moment after you made it. That medicine just…dissolved them. Your parents and I had a plan before I even found you. If you were alive, they would move far away and start over, just in case IESS ever came looking for you again. But Shalene Dunleavy had all this news coverage around your disappearance, so your parents changed your name to protect you from that."

"So, I'm not even from North Carolina. I'm from here? My whole life, all of my memories were from here? I didn't fall down a ravine, I was fucking kidnapped?" She backed away from him, so angry and hurt her head spun.

"Don't leave." His voice came out a desperate snarl, and his eyes were the color of snow.

"Clinton!" Harrison called from the entrance of the park. The other Boarlanders were behind him, looking concerned, and Alyssa or Shae or whoever the fuck she was couldn't do this in front of them.

"I'm going back home."

"I'll come with you."

"Not to your trailer park. I'm going back to North Carolina. I need space."

"No, no, no, no," Clinton chanted in quick succession. "Shae." Clinton's voice sounded strangled, and then there was a popping sound behind her.

Horrified, she turned, but she couldn't

make sense of what she saw. Clinton was on his hands and knees, his shoulder crunching and his spine elongating. His eyes were terrified, and when he opened his mouth to speak, his teeth were longer and sharper. "Run."

She must've misheard him. A minute ago, he'd told her not to run, and now he was changing his mind? He was breaking. She'd done this. She had to help. To save him somehow. "What do I do?"

"Shae," he said, leveling her with those fierce eyes. "Ruuuun!" His voice tapered into a roar as a massive, blond grizzly exploded from his body. The bear stumbled toward her, as if he was fighting his steps.

"Oh, my God," she whispered as she stared at the slowly approaching predator. His jerky footfall was so hard it vibrated the ground under her feet.

His silver eyes lifted from the long, curved claws on his feet to her, and there was a moment of regret that pooled there in the mercury. But in a flash, he blinked, and then there was nothing but determination in his wild gaze. And the next step he took was deliberate.

Clinton was coming for her.

She spun and bolted toward her car, yanking her keys out of her back pocket. She fumbled for the right one. Damn keychains! Why did she need all these cutsie, jingling *obstacles*? No time to reach the driver's side, she aimed for the passenger's side. A horrified sound wrenched from her throat as she dropped her keys into the grass.

She stumbled to a stop, off balance and going down to her hands and feet to turn for the keychain. She gripped clumps of wild grass to help with traction, but Harrison was screaming now. "Don't stop, Alyssa. Go!"

Clinton was getting closer, ducking and dodging parked cars, his eyes glued to her. He was hunting.

With a terrified gasp, she heeded the alpha's demand, spun back around and sprinted for the woods behind the parking lot, pushing her legs faster than she ever had in her life. In the distance, over the trees, a wall of storm clouds ghosted the horizon, lightning flashing in the darkening sky.

She was small enough to fit through the space between cars, but not Clinton. He was having to swerve into empty spaces and it was buying her time. When she dared a look to her left, Bash was keeping pace with her fifteen cars down. Her next glance over and he was a pitch black grizzly. An earth shattering roar sounded from behind her, and then another answered. Now the Boarlanders were hunting her, too.

No. She looked over at Bash as he pushed toward her through the thinning cars. His furious gaze wasn't on her. It was behind her—on Clinton. They were trying to help her. She had to believe that right now.

Gritting her teeth, she pushed her legs harder. She had to buy them time to cut him off. Her thighs burned, and her lungs were on fire. The terror had done something awful to her chest, making the air she dragged in with every pant too thick.

She was so close to the tree line now, but the grass was un-mowed and taller, so she had to lift her knees higher. Clinton was right behind her. She could hear him breathing, hear the snarl in his chest that punched with every breath. She could hear his massive paws flattening the grass, and she imagined his breath on the back of her neck.

She was going to be killed by the one she loved.

Muscles burning, Alyssa pushed through the first row of trees and took off at an angle, but her sneaker caught a loop of tree root, and she screamed as she went down hard. She rolled over just in time to see Clinton bearing down on her with such speed and such precision, there would be no surviving this. And behind him came a herd of monsters.

Everything slowed.

A giant black boar with blazing blue eyes and long, razor sharp tusks.

Bash's black grizzly.

A brown bear with fire in his eyes, mouth open as he gained on Clinton.

An enormous silverback gorilla, charging closer to Clinton with long, powerful arms, his smooth black lips curled back over long canines.

A white tiger, snarling in an expression that promised pain. Audrey. She was trying to save Alyssa, too, but they were all too late. She wouldn't get to say goodbye to her friends.

And in that moment, something became clear to her.

I want to hurt you. I want to bite you. Clinton had tried to warn her away, and she hadn't listened.

"Clinton, don't!" Alyssa screamed as he skidded to a stop over her, paws bigger than her face on either side of her head. Tears streamed out from corners of her eyes as she locked gazes with him. There was no hesitation as he curled his lips back, exposing impossibly long, sharp teeth. And then he clamped his jaw over her shoulder.

The pain was excruciating. She shrieked, waiting for him to shake her and tear her limb from limb, but as quickly as he'd slammed those powerful jaws down around her flesh, he released her.

And then everything resumed real time when Clinton was blasted sideways. The Boarlanders had him. Ripping, shredding, clawing, snarling, roaring. They all fought like injured animals, driven by desperation.

Clinton was winning. He was pushing them back toward her. Audrey was thrown off. Kirk, too. Clinton in all his rage was coming back to finish her off.

Clutching her bleeding shoulder, she winced at the pain that rippled down every nerve ending in her body. Her blood was boiling, her veins exploding with the heat. Alyssa retched and struggled to sit up.

Kill me.

It would be easier to die than endure this pain. To endure the betrayal. To endure an empty life where she didn't know who she was.

She sat on her knees in the shade of the evergreens, her yellow Team Clinton shirt turning crimson. She dared a look at her shoulder and gagged again. Her skin was tattered, hanging in strips and gushing, but that wasn't the most terrifying thing. A soft rumble bellowed up from her like a demon escaping hell.

"Let him alone!" she screamed at Bash and Mason.

The boar and the black grizzly disengaged and backed off as she stood. Fury fed her now, and it was a helluva lot more powerful with all this adrenaline dumping into her dying system.

"If anyone is going to bleed this asshole, it'll be me." Her voice sounded like a monster.

Ally appeared through the trees, hands out in a soothing gesture, but fuck that.

"Don't come any closer," Alyssa snarled.

Ally froze like the smart woman she was, and the Boarlanders backed away slowly.

"Alyssa," Ally pleaded, "don't kill him."

Kill him? She was small and frail. She'd been running from a predator a minute ago. She had blunt nails and blunt teeth and was no match for Clinton the fucking grizzly bear. All she had was rage. And that rage was so deep and so wide that it bellowed up from her like magma spewing from a volcano. Alyssa closed her eyes against the pain, allowing the anger to burst out of her.

She inhaled quick and screamed a horrifying sound that tapered into a roar and then into a long growl. With a rumble in her chest, she landed on four feet and stared down in horror at her giant paws. Long, curved claws had replaced her useless fingernails, and her paws were massive as she flattened them against the earth. Fur covered her body, black on the coarse under-layer and lightening to a dove gray on top. She could smell everything. She could smell the fear wafting from the Boarlanders, acrid and bitter against her new nose. She could hear their pounding heartbeats and see every defined strand of fur on their bodies. Power rippled through her in a wave as she swung her furious gaze to Clinton.

He'd been hers, and look what he'd done. He'd claimed her, put a bear in her, and all without her consent. *Consent*—that word had meant so much to him, and now this?

Alyssa hated what he'd done.

Clinton was a full-grown, mature bruin,

blond fur waving in the early storm winds. His eyes were blazing silver as he raked his gaze appraisingly over her body, but she wasn't flattered. Not now. Not when he'd forced this after all his lies and betrayal.

On top of everything, he'd stolen her humanity.

She bunched her muscles and charged, power pulsing through her body with every step. She was fucking invincible in this body, fueled by her anger. So fast, she barreled down on him. The surrounding forest blurred to nothing but an ugly patchwork of brown and green as she leapt through the air.

Clinton caught her full in the chest and was rammed backward against a massive tree trunk. She clawed and bit and slapped and bled him without pity because he deserved to be punished. The dull sensation of pain on her shoulder was annoying, but nothing more. The Boarlanders backed away. They were going to let her have this kill. They were letting her have vengeance.

Why wasn't Clinton fighting back?

He was ducking her, trying to escape her death blows, trying to protect his neck from her canines. Coward. Coward! She wished she had her human voice so she could tell him how sad he'd made her. How angry. But since she didn't, she could only tell him with pain.

The air smelled like iron, and her paws were wet. Clinton's fur was matted and splattered with crimson, and now she felt sick. Sick, sick, sick. Sick of fighting. Sick of hurting. With a strange, long sob, she went limp on top of him and hoped the Boarlanders killed her because she'd hurt him.

Him.

She'd hurt her mate, her love. Clinton threw his arm over her back, and there was a long, soft rumbling sound coming from his chest. She didn't know how she knew, but she did. It was the sound of mourning. So she matched it with a heartbroken sound of her own.

The Fates had given them to each other so young, and what had she and Clinton done with that time?

They'd ruined each other.

Her body broke and shrunk. Muscles reshaped, bones snapped, and pain rippled through her body in tsunami waves. She fell backward as Clinton took his human form. It looked painful, and she grimaced away from the sight. That's what she looked like now.

The Boarlanders looked so sad. So sad.

Everything felt surreal as Alyssa rested on her folded legs in the dirt. Warmth streamed from her body, but she stared in horror as a long gash on her arm shrank, then closed up completely. There was that shifter healing. Shifter. She was one of them now. Them. A sob wrenched through her as she wrapped her arms around her middle. She was shivering. So cold.

There was a man in the woods with a phone pointed at her, but Harrison was human again and to him in a moment. He took the phone from him and slammed it against a tree. His bare body was rigid as he yelled at the stranger. "Have some respect! She's naked, you asshole!"

Naked. Alyssa looked down at her bare skin, and twin tears rolled down her cheeks.

"I'm sorry," Clinton said, his voice breaking on the apology as he rocked on his knees in the dirt.

His eyes were so raw, and he smelled of something new. Regret? Guilt? Unhappiness to be sure.

Her shoulders shook, and a whimper clawed up her throat. Even after everything, the thought of hurting him made her sick. But this had to be said because he'd done something really, horribly bad.

In a strangled whisper, she told him, "You aren't forgiven."

SIXTEEN

Alyssa ran her finger across the scar on the outside of her big toe—the scar she'd gotten the day she'd been taken. Taken from Saratoga, taken from Clinton, taken from her parents, taken from her life. She hadn't ever noticed it before, but now it was there, more proof she was Shae.

Such a hollowness filled her middle, and now she felt as if she were hovering just outside of her body. She was nothing more than a lost balloon floating toward the sun. What a lonely feeling.

Her bear rumbled inside of her, but she was getting used to that. Two days of self-banishment in 1010 with nothing but her bear to talk to, and they were getting to know each other quite well.

Harrison had called her "dominant" on the

way to the trailer park from the Lumberjack Wars. She'd told the Boarlanders she wanted to go home, but Harrison said she couldn't. Not until she had control of her bear. He said, for now, Boarland Mobile Park had to be her home.

Another knock sounded on her door, but she ignored it like all the rest. She didn't want to be talked down from feeling. From coping. She wanted to think about all of this in private. Wanted to mourn the loss of her humanity, the loss of herself, the loss of her name and her hometown and her story, all if it.

Her phone sat face up on the laminate wood flooring in front of her. She was sitting under the AC unit in 1010 because the droning sound calmed her animal for some reason.

Mom was calling again.

Feeling numb, Alyssa reached for it and accepted the call.

"Alyssa? Are you there?"

"When you call me that name, it sounds like more lies."

Mom went quiet for a minute, and then softly she said, "Would you like me to call you Shae?"

"I don't know." Alyssa shook her head helplessly. "I don't know anything."

"Baby, can I just explain?" Mom was crying. Alyssa could hear it in her voice. She was trying to be strong and steady, but that little tremor and sniff gave her away.

"Sure." Alyssa's voice sounded hollow, even to herself.

"It wasn't like we planned on never telling you. That's not how it started out. But you're our only daughter, and when you were taken, it was awful. Clinton came back from the woods, half-dead, panicked, screaming about how someone took you. I was in shock. He had been beaten so badly, I barely recognized his face, and he was saying you were gone. Just...gone. His parents wanted to move him away to protect him in case the IESS came back, but he wouldn't leave us." Mom's voice upped an octave, and she sniffed a few times before she continued. "He wouldn't leave us. And the police were telling us that after forty-eight hours, the chances of finding you alive were slim, but every time, your dad and I started to think 'what if?' What if you were dead? Clinton was right there, telling us you didn't feel dead to him. And he was bonded to you, baby. He had this instinct we couldn't understand, but he was sure. He was so sure you were still out there somewhere. And so we went to work. Dad quit his job to track you full time, and Clinton dropped out of school. He was going to these terrifying, dark places to gather information, and every time he left I was so afraid we would lose him, too, and his parents would have to go through the same thing that we were. But he never gave up on you. Never. Not for a moment. And when he found you, baby…when he negotiated for you, he knew there was no way he was coming back out of there, but it didn't matter to him. He was so happy. He was hugging us, crying, promising us he would get you back safe, but we had to take care. Once he went in and took your place, we had nothing to bargain with anymore. So we had to keep you safe, change your name, and move. We started a whole new life, terrified every day they would come back for you."

Alyssa cupped her hand over her mouth as her shoulders shook and tears streamed down her face. For two days, she'd thought about how this all affected her, but she hadn't realized how hard it had been on her parents, or on Clinton. It didn't excuse the lies, but it made her understand them better.

"We were going to tell you when Clinton escaped. He called us on the road, and we were so happy he was alive. So happy he was out, but there was something wrong with him. He sounded different. He wasn't…" Mom blew out a long breath. "He wasn't okay to come back for you. They'd done something awful to him in there that took that boy away from us, away from his parents, and away from you. He said he wished he'd died in there." Mom sobbed, and her voice thickened. "And your dad and I could tell he meant it with all his heart, and you had been in there for the same amount of time, enduring God-knows-what, but you were okay. You weren't using drugs to cope with that awful time, or drinking, or hating yourself or hating the world. You weren't having to deal with any of that because you didn't have any memory of it. And we wanted to *keep* you. Dad and I wanted to keep you safe from what Clinton was going through, and he wanted the same, so we kept up the lie. We weren't trying to hurt you, baby. We were trying to save you."

"I'm sorry, Mom. I'm sorry it happened, and I'm sorry you had to make all those hard decisions. Please forgive me."

"For what, Alyssa? You did nothing wrong."

"For putting you and dad through that. I

can't imagine how scared you must've been. Two years!" She shrugged and looked up at the sagging ceiling of 1010. "Thank you for not giving up on me."

"Never. We would never. You'll always be our little girl." Mom swallowed hard. "Clinton told us what he did to you."

"Mom—"

"No, you listen. I know you're mad at him. I *know* it. He didn't go about it the right way, but you should know that bear in your middle was always the plan."

"Whose plan?"

"Yours. You and Clinton were bonded early when you were just little kids. And oh, it terrified your dad and me. Watching you fall so hard for a boy with a bear in him? But as the years went on, and we saw Clinton's character, how he took care of you, stuck up for you at school, was so devoted to you, and pushed you to be better, to be stronger… He became a son we'd never had. And we were glad he picked you, and that you picked him back because he was so steadfast. I even had a dress picked out for your wedding because I just knew I was gonna be the mother of the bride as soon as you two turned eighteen. You were just so confident in him, and you always had great taste in people. You told us when you were fourteen that someday Clinton would claim you, and you would be like him. You told us you two were already talking about it, but he wanted to wait until you were older so that the bear wouldn't scare you. He wanted to give you time to be human. You would come home so angry." Mom laughed thickly. "It was all you fought about. You two got along so well, but you would get mad because he was putting off Turning you. But I knew it wasn't because he didn't want to claim you. He just wanted to make it special. And he's gutted now because he failed at that. He didn't do it the right way, but you have to realize, he's waited his whole life for that moment. If his bear was still okay, and if he hadn't gone into that damned facility, he would've made it a beautiful declaration for you. But his bear got scared of losing you, and Clinton couldn't help himself. You've known you loved him for a few weeks, but that boy, that man, has loved you with everything he has since he was ten. Please, honey, for your sake and for his, give him a chance to explain himself."

Alyssa heaved a sigh and hugged the phone closer to her ear. "Okay, mom."

"I love you, baby."

Her lips twitched up in the first smile in days. "I love you, too."

And when she hung up, she rested her head back against the wall and tracked Nards's progress over her leg and into the bathroom. The little field mouse with the giant testicles had a potato chip in his mouth, bringing dinner back for his lady mouse, Nipples.

Another knock sounded at the front door, and this time she didn't ignore it.

This time, she got up and wiped her cheeks and straightened her spine. It was time to stop feeling sorry for herself and face the outside world.

It was time to move on.

SEVENTEEN

Alyssa pushed the door open, but Clinton wasn't standing there like she thought he would be. He was sitting with his back to her on the top porch stair, as if he hadn't expected her to answer. It was pouring rain, and his white T-shirt was soaked through, but that wasn't the most heartbreaking part of seeing him again. There was a soggy mattress on her porch, right by the door as though he'd been sleeping in the downpour that had soaked Damon's mountains over the last two days. There was no comforter or pillow.

Clinton's shoulders were rigid from shivering, and when he turned around, his eyes were so full of raw heartache, it nearly buckled her knees.

After everything, how had they gotten here?

Clinton stood slowly. His shirt clung to his body, so see-through she could make out every muscle, tensed against the shaking. But she could see something more as well—the scars her bear had given him. They were red, angry, and raised all along his throat and torso. His eyes were silver and churned like the storm clouds above him. She'd seen the same color in her own eyes in the mirror…because he was her maker.

He backed down the stairs, chin lowered, gaze on her legs, neck exposed. He was giving her space. She was glad. She was heartbroken. All these different emotions roiled around inside of her like a tornado. What was she supposed to feel now? Anger? Gratefulness? Surely not this empty feeling that had consumed her.

"I have to show you something," he said low.

Lightning flashed behind his shoulders, and thunder boomed. Although she jumped hard at the loud sound that rang against her newly sensitive eardrums, Clinton didn't react at all. He just looked broken.

"What is it?" she asked.

"It won't make up for what I've done, but maybe it'll help fill in some of the blanks of your story." He opened his mouth like he meant to say more, but closed it again and ducked his gaze to the ground. He pulled a folded piece of paper from his back pocket and set it onto the wet porch railing, then tried to smile and strode toward his trailer.

Slowly, Alyssa made her way down the stairs and unfolded the note. It was an address.

The blue ink was wet and smeared, but still readable.

1414 LAKE RANCH ROAD, SARATOGA, WY

"Clinton?"

He hunched his shoulders and turned in the rain, neck still exposed.

"What is this?"

"Your childhood home. I bought it because…"

"Because what?"

He gritted his teeth, his jaw clenching hard. "I bought it because I wanted to be close to you. And because I wanted to remember what it felt like to be okay."

She clutched the precious note to her chest and hesitated with her response, hoping desperately her voice would come out stronger than she felt. "Will you take me?"

When his blazing eyes jerked to hers, he

looked so uncertain. "I swear I won't hurt you. I won't hurt you again. You'll be safe in the truck with me."

"I know. Go put dry clothes on. I don't want you getting sick."

"I won't get sick."

"Clinton, I have all these instincts now. And I'm really confused about where we stand, but I know I can't watch you shiver like that anymore."

He dipped his head once, then disappeared inside his trailer while she made her way to his truck.

"Am I your mate?" she asked, the second he slipped behind the wheel of his truck.

Clinton froze, gaze averted, and with a huffed breath, he nodded.

"Since when?"

"Since we were ten."

Alyssa could hear lies now. It was one of the growing list of things she liked about her bear, though she wasn't quite ready to tell Clinton 'thank you' for giving her to Alyssa. He'd still gone about it wrong. Clinton had been telling the truth. Age ten. Eighteen years she'd been Clinton's mate, but for the life of her, she couldn't remember their youth other than those two dreams. She felt robbed. He had all these memories that bound him to her, but she had so few. Sure, he still felt like everything good in her life, but she didn't have the history or the context he did.

It wasn't fair.

Clinton was so quiet on the way to Saratoga, Alyssa turned up a country station on the radio just to drown out the heavy silence. He normally drove like a maniac, but today he drove slowly, coasting each corner.

"Why?" she asked.

"Because you'll leave soon, and I don't want to rush my time with you."

The agony in his voice had settled an ache in her stomach that made her keep her questions to herself for the rest of the trip. And when he took a right onto Lake Ranch Road, Alyssa leaned forward in her seat, desperate to have some memory sparked from this place.

There was nothing, though. No recognition at all. The memories just weren't there, didn't exist anymore. They'd been burned away with whatever medicine those awful people had given her.

Clinton pulled up to an old, dilapidated house. It had been painted white at one point, but now the paint had chipped on the wood siding and given way to rot. The roof sagged, and the old fence out back had been knocked over. But the yard stunned her. There were thousands of dandelion weeds, all topped with yellow flowers.

The other yards in the neighborhood were mowed and pretty, but here, there was no grass. Only flowers.

"I planted them," Clinton murmured as he watched her.

"You planted weeds? Why?"

"You'll see. Stay there, and I'll get your door."

Clinton jogged around the front, shoulders hunched against the rain, then opened her door and folded her in his arms. She didn't ask to be carried across the mud and weeds, but as she stretched her toes out, she realized she hadn't put on shoes when she left. Carefully, she slid her arms around his neck, and Clinton brushed his jaw against the top of her hair, as if he couldn't help the affection.

There was an official note from the city on the front door telling Clinton he needed to take care of his yard, but he just ripped it down and threw it in a pile of papers just inside the door.

He set her down on the dusty wooden

floors and backed away a few feet, giving her space. He looked at her so expectantly she had to come clean. With a shake of her head, she whispered, "Nothing."

"That's okay." He slid his big hand around hers and led her to a small bedroom. She looked behind her at the footprints she'd made in the dust, right next to his giant boot prints. The light in here was muted and natural, streaming through the windows. The rafters on the ceiling of the room were covered in cobwebs, and one of the windows had a long crack. Water sounded—*drip, drip, drip*—off the windowsill and onto the floor that had been warped from long-term water damage.

Clinton sat against the wall, drew his knees up, and rested his arms over them. He twitched his chin at the center of the room where there was no dust around one of the floorboards. Slowly, she padded over to it and sank down to her knees. And then she pried the loose board up easily. Inside was a half-full bottle of whiskey and a colorful diary.

And still...there was nothing.

Alyssa opened it to the first page.

Shalene Dawn Dunleavy – age ten
Mom told me she used to write her

adventures in a journal, and so she bought one for me for my birthday. I don't really know what to say in these things. Oh, well I found a kitten the other day by an old barn in the woods and mom said we could keep it. He doesn't have a tail and he is black. I know lots of people say black cats are bad luck, but that isn't true, so I named him Lucky. I have to bottle feed him every few hours. He is so cute.

Below that, there was a terrible drawing of a cat without a tail. Alyssa huffed a surprised laugh. She recognized those wonky eyes. Here was her signature shitty drawing skills, displayed at age ten.

Enamored, she turned the page.

Clinton said he loves me today…
I cried and then forgot to say it back and now he probably thinks I'm mean and I'm a crybaby. I'm not. I just got excited. I'm going to tell him soon, no matter what.

Tonight, Clinton came and asked if I could go out into the woods with him because he had a surprise. Mom let me, even though it was a school night. I don't get scared in the woods because Clinton is special and would never let anything happen to me. He's stronger than anyone. We caught fireflies and put them in a jar and brought them back for Mom and she smiled really big. I didn't tell her, but Clinton kissed me out there. It was like a peck, but soft and it made my stomach feel funny, but in a good way. I told him I love him too.

A couple months passed before the next entry. Alyssa lost herself in her life story. It was like a book, but better, because she'd written it for her eyes only, uncensored, and now she was getting this amazing look at herself she never thought she would have.

Age Eleven

Clinton is doing bad in school. He tries but he has trouble with his attention, so I'm helping him learn after school. I love his family. They always let me come over and his mom is a really good cook. She makes food that makes people happy to sit around the table and talk. I always get this good feeling when I eat dinner with them, even though his brothers are really annoying and make kissing noises at me and Clinton. On Friday, Mrs. Fuller taught me how to make cracker crumb chicken, and now maybe I want to be a chef when I grow up. I want to make people feel good when they eat dinner together too.

Alyssa shook her head and dared a look at Clinton. "I love cooking."

He offered her a lopsided smile. "You and my mom were magic in the kitchen. You two were always cookin' up something good. She always wanted a daughter, but got all boys who didn't give a shit about making food. But you spent the time with her. I called her the other day and told her you'd claimed me, and she cried for a long time. My family wants to see you if you're ever ready."

Alyssa nodded. "I'd like that."

She made her way to Clinton and rested her head in his lap, then read the next entry out loud as he stroked her hair. "Clinton got me a ring for Christmas and told me it was a promise ring. It turned my finger green but I don't care. We didn't tell anyone at school what it means, but we know. Someday, I'm going to be Shalene Fuller and wear a big white sparkly dress. Or maybe I'll make him be Clinton Dunleavy." She'd doodled both names onto the bottom of that sheet in curly, swirly letters.

Alyssa giggled and kept reading. She read page after page, year after year as she got to know herself through her own youthful eyes. And she noticed similarities. She still had the same wit and found the same humor funny. She still liked the same kind of music and wished her hair was more manageable.

An entry at age fourteen took her a while to get through. It talked about her conversations with Clinton and wanting him to Turn her so she could be like him, so she could be his forever. She cried at that part. Clinton looked gutted and stared out the window, shaking his head like it was too much. But she got through it and went on to the next entry, which was about a concert she and Clinton had gone to with his brothers and how annoying they'd been. It was a fun one to follow the heartbreak. It was the comic relief she'd needed to regain her composure and push on.

Age sixteen

Alyssa pulled off a plastic bag that had been taped over the entry. Inside was an old, dried dandelion flower.

Aloud, she read, "The other day, Clinton gave me this flower. It's yellow, my favorite color, and he said it was so pretty that it reminded him of me. He's never given me a flower before, so I dried it in between the pages of my math book and put it here. I'm going to keep it forever. He told me, 'Look for me in the dandelions,' because if I ever saw that flower, that was his love for me." Alyssa's voice dipped to nothing. Her lip trembled, and she snuggled her face against Clinton's thigh.

She taped the flower back to the page and turned to the next. It was blank.

"You were taken a few days after this," he said in a hoarse voice. "That was your last entry."

She could see something written through the thin paper, so she turned to the next page. This one was written in black ink and neat, small, capital letters. It matched the handwriting on the address Clinton had given her today.

I'm back here, but not really. It's been years since I've been in this house, and I thought I would feel happy here again. I hoped. I swear I can almost smell her scent still lingering on these old walls, but I know I'm just imagining it. Shae is just a ghost and so am I.

Next page.

I got weak and spent three paychecks traveling out to North Carolina to see her. Creed was pissed that I ditched the Gray Backs mid logging season for a random vacation. When I saw her, I thought about introducing myself, but I hate everyone after Amber. I don't want to hate Shae. I just watched her work at this diner for hours, just stared at her through the window and felt like my heart was being ripped out of my chest. She's way too good for the man I've become.

Selfish Monster. Leave her alone.

After that entry, they all ended with that tagline. *Selfish Monster. Leave her alone.* Alyssa closed the diary because she couldn't read anymore of his pain and be okay. Not now. She wasn't ready, wasn't strong enough yet.

"I bought this place a few years ago," he explained. "I was hoping your parents didn't know about the diary and hadn't taken it with them when they moved because I wanted it. I wanted that piece of you. Wanted the reminders about how much you had cared about me once. The Boarlanders don't know I own this place, so I come out here when everything gets too heavy. And I drink and read your journal and remember the good parts before Amber got to me. I remember you because you are all my good parts." Clinton scrubbed his hand down his beard, and his eyes rimmed with moisture. "I'm sorry I broke you, too. I'm so sorry."

Alyssa sat up and straddled him, melted against his chest and hugged him hard. "I didn't know it was like this for you. I didn't know I was already yours or that you were already mine. I'm angry that you scared me, but I understand. You were scared to lose me again."

Clinton kissed the side of her head, let his lips linger there for a long time as he held her tightly against him. "I was *terrified* of losing you. It's not an excuse, though. I can't stop thinking about you running from me and not being able to stop my bear. I can't stop seeing the fear in your eyes when I bit you. And now this…" He eased back and cupped her face. He brushed the pads of his thumbs right under her eyes. "You're so goddamned beautiful, but the silver in your eyes will always remind me of what I did to you."

A warm tear streaked down her cheek as she kissed the palm of his hand. "Listen to me." She held his gaze so he could see her honesty, as well as hear it. "I forgive you."

"Don't let me off the hook—"

"I do. I forgive you for all of it. I know you were trying to protect me. And I saw you trying to stop your bear. These silver eyes? They were always meant to be mine, Clinton Fuller. Do you hear me? *Always*. We just took a really long, broken road to get here. I don't regret the bear you gave me. I love her. Now that I know how we were, what I'd wanted, how scared you were to lose me, I *love* her. Come here."

She tugged his hand upward and led him out of the bedroom, traced their steps in the dust until they were standing on the front porch of her childhood home. She stared out at the yard full of weeds.

Look for me in the dandelions.

Alyssa stood on her tiptoes and kissed his lips softly. And then she eased back and hugged him close, her eyes on the sea of yellow flowers. "I forgive you because you never gave up on me, even when you'd given up on yourself."

EIGHTEEN

It was dark by the time they got back to Boarland Mobile Park. Someone had turned on the strands of outdoor lights that lit up the trailer park at night, and such a strange feeling washed through Alyssa when she saw 1010 at the end of the road. That old trailer felt like home now. So much had happened here.

She'd found Clinton again.

She'd found friends in the Boarlanders and the other crews in Damon's mountains.

She'd gotten a job managing Moosey's and would soon have a pet baby mouse when Nipples weaned her little peanut. The boys had already bullied her into naming it Tittycakes.

But the biggest thing—she'd figured out who she was here. And no, that didn't mean Shalene Dawn Dunleavy either. She'd discovered who she—Alyssa—was.

"I've thought about what you asked."

"Okay," Clinton said, pulling to a stop in front of his trailer. "What name do I call you?"

"You know how you were upset I kept mentioning the boy from my dreams because you didn't want me comparing you to the boy you used to be?"

Clinton nodded, a slow smile spreading across his face. It was the big genuine one where she could see his teeth. The one that reached his eyes and stopped her breath. God, he was so handsome. His eyes were that gray, happy color, and the feral edge had disappeared from his facial features. His muscular chest rose slowly as he put the truck into park and draped his arm over the steering wheel.

"I feel the same. I don't know myself as Shae, and I don't want you comparing me to a person I don't remember. I want you to fall for me. I want you to call me Alyssa."

His grin turned soft, and he leaned over and sipped at her lips. Alyssa let off a sigh and wrapped her arms around him. She smiled against his lips and murmured, "Say it."

Clinton nipped her bottom lip, his teeth grazing her skin in a delicious tease. Instead of minding though, Clinton got that stubborn look and got out of the truck. He yanked her door open and pulled her out onto the wet gravel. When her bare feet sank into the mud, she laughed. Clinton's eyes were glued to the curve of her lips for a moment before he threw her over his shoulder and jogged up the stairs of his trailer.

At the door, he settled her on her feet and cupped her neck, then kissed her again, harder this time. He pushed his tongue past her lips and shoved open the door, guided her backward into his house. Her muddy feet slipped on the wood floors, but he kept her upright. Upright. He'd somehow always done that.

"Say it, Clinton," she growled. She squeaked and clapped her hands over her mouth in embarrassment.

Clinton swatted her hands away and let off a louder growl. "Don't hide your animal from me, woman. You're sexy as hell, all snarly and badass, smelling like fur and arousal."

"Show me what I did to you."

Clinton narrowed his eyes but complied. He pulled his shirt over his head, and damn. He bore light scars from all his scuffles with the Gray Backs and Boarlanders and from the boar war, but none of those compared to the raised marks over his body now.

He wore a sexy smirk. "Beast," he accused.

"I don't regret it."

His wicked grin grew bigger. "Not even a little?"

Alyssa traced the bite mark on his shoulder, then ran her finger along some of the claw marks on his neck and chest made by her paws. "No one will miss my claiming marks now," she whispered.

The smile dipped from Clinton's face, and his lips collided with hers. He was everywhere, everything. Air and warmth, safety. Her mate. The snarl in her throat was back as she dipped her fingertips below the waist of his jeans. When she brushed the top of his hard cock, his hips jerked.

She'd never felt more empowered. Now no one stood a chance of taking her, or hurting her, because she wielded a beast, created from Clinton's monster grizzly. And now she had Clinton with a touch.

His fingertips dug hard into her hips, and she loved it. Loved him wild and reckless. They didn't have to be gentle with each other anymore because he'd banished Amber's ghost, and now Alyssa was an apex predator shifter like him.

Frantic, she shoved his pants down his legs and shimmied out of her own. Clinton ripped her shirt down the front and shoved the tatters off her shoulders, then unsnapped her bra like he'd done it a hundred times. Maybe he had when they were younger, who knew? She loved their history now, even if she didn't remember every moment. Their bond was bone-deep and all-consuming, and how lucky that she'd found that after everything that had happened.

She took a long stroke of Clinton's thick shaft, and he pushed his tongue back into her mouth, over and over, matching the pace she set. He walked her backward until her back was against the wall, and he rolled his hips hard against hers, hitting her just right.

"Please," she begged shamelessly. Yesterday she'd thought she was losing him and everything she loved, but today had opened her eyes to so much. She didn't have to give him up. This was her second chance at happiness, and she was so damn relieved they were here, in this moment.

Clinton pulled her hand off his dick and shoved her knees farther apart with his. And then he dipped the head of his shaft into her slick entrance. On the second thrust, he buried himself deeply inside of her and let off a groan that matched the relief she felt. He pulled out slow and rammed into her again. Alyssa threw her head back in disbelief that anything could feel this good, this right. He lifted the back of her knee until her leg was hooked around his waist, and he went at her like a rutting animal, faster and harder as she cried out his name. His abs were like steel against her stomach as he flexed on each thrust, and there were his teeth, gentle on the long scars where he'd torn into her shoulder. Where he'd Turned her. Where he'd claimed he didn't want anyone but her.

She clawed his back and gritted out, "Say it."

And as he slid into her and froze, his dick throbbing the first shot of warmth into her, he growled out the word she'd been waiting so long to hear. "Alyssa."

Orgasm blasted through her, matching his pulsing release as he picked up an erratic pace and slid into her again and again. When he emptied himself completely, he murmured it softer. "Alyssa."

And then he eased back and cupped her face, uncertainty in his eyes. "I'll get better. I'll be better for you."

She shook her head and eased him back so he could see her face better. She knew her eyes were bright silver to match his right now. "I don't want you to change. I like you just like this. Wild, stubborn, caring, funny, sensitive man. I like that I get to see your secret side. I like that I'm the only one you give it to."

Clinton nuzzled his rough beard down one side of her face and then down the other, and she got it. She was a bear now and understood the affection. She understood the *thank you*.

"I'm scared of Changing," she whispered as the vibration in her chest became uncomfortable. Her bear needed something she didn't understand.

"I don't want you to be scared of anything."

"Then teach me."

Clinton's answering smile was breathtaking. He scooped her up, just like he had in her dream when she'd cut her foot. And then he took her outside and didn't stop walking until he reached the Boarlander woods. In the dark shadows of the night forest, he settled her on her feet and squared up to her, so tall and powerful. She was powerful now, too, if only she could figure out how to harness it. She'd been afraid to Change again because of the pain.

"Don't fight her," he murmured. He nipped at her neck, then sucked hard, drawing a gasp from Alyssa. "When she feels like she's filling you up, close your eyes and let her have your skin." Clinton walked backward, his eyes reflecting like an animal's in the muted light from the trailer park. A proud smile curved his lips. "Alyssa?"

"Yes?"

"I've never seen a grizzly like yours. Dominant, brawling, badass. Gray like your eyes with that pitch-black undercoat. You're so beautiful."

She clenched her hands at her sides as pain boiled through her middle again. There she was—her animal. *Hers*. Pride surged through her.

Clinton hunched inward, and his blond bear blasted from his skin in an instant. And when he landed on all fours and shook his head, she closed her eyes and imagined herself a bear. And with a massive wave of pain, she broke apart and reshaped into something other. Something better. She reshaped into her new self. Alyssa, mate of Clinton, the last bear of the Boarlander crew, the last mate of Damon's mountains.

Clinton rubbed his giant body down her side and then lifted his big head to the clouds and roared a deafening sound. This wasn't angry. It wasn't a warning. It was an invitation.

He was calling the Boarlanders.

He was calling their crew.

The woods went quiet, and the wind died down, and then there was a loud, echoing drum. Kirk was beating his chest. *I'm coming. Wait for me.*

She understood so much more in this form.

The call of a big cat filled the woods, followed by the roar of a bear and then another. And when she turned, Mason was there, an enormous black boar, head high, ears erect. Bash charged through the woods and play swatted her on his way by. Alyssa huffed a laugh and ducked out of the way, hooked a paw at his back leg until he stumbled. Audrey's white tiger contrasted against the dark night, and she snarled up one side of her mouth, exposing one canine. She rubbed her body up one side of Alyssa's body and down the other. She rubbed her fur the wrong way, but that was okay.

Ally and Emerson appeared beside each other, and Beck too, holding a sleeping Air-

Ryder on her hip. The girls were all smiling through their tears. How could crying look so happy?

And then Harrison's dark brown bear was there, eyes on her from where he stood on the outskirts of the greeting. He let off a long roar, his breath frozen in front of his muzzle, and it filled Alyssa with an urge to join in. So she did. She lifted her chin and gave her voice to the chorus, and there was pride in Clinton's blazing silver eyes.

With a powerful stride, Harrison sauntered up to her, and buried his nose against the scruff of Alyssa's neck as if memorizing her scent.

She exposed her throat and dipped her head. *Alpha*. Harrison deserved respect.

Bash followed directly behind Harrison, and Audrey playfully leapt on his back before sliding down and falling into line beside him. Mason trotted quietly through the brush, and Kirk jumped for a branch, then swung up beside the boar. The women hiked after the others, and then Clinton followed them, but glanced at Alyssa over his shoulder, waiting.

These were her people now. Her Boarlanders. Her crew.

And Clinton was her mate. And she

belonged, which felt like such a big deal after carrying such hollowness for so long.

How had she gotten so damn lucky?

Rumbling out a content growl, Alyssa pushed her new body forward and walked alongside the bear shifter who had given her everything. Who had sacrificed himself so that she was here to own this moment, safe and whole.

She wasn't Shae Dunleavy anymore.

She was Alyssa of the Boarlanders.

EPILOGUE

"How am I this big already?" Willa groused, resting a plate of loaded fries covered in what smelled like pickle juice onto the swell of her stomach.

Alyssa slurped down the rest of her Long Island Iced Tea. "Not big, just carrying multiples."

"This is all your fault," Willa said, pointing an accusing french fry at her mate, Matt.

Matt looked proud as hell as he reclined back on two legs of his chair in Sammy's bar. "What can I say? My sperm is potent."

"I want a second opinion," Willa said around a giant bite, twitching her dyed red hair out of the way. "I swear I'm carrying a litter of bears, a dozen at least."

"Just two," Matt said. "I'll try to put more in you next time."

"Next time?" Willa asked. "Fuck no, you're never getting near my snake-hole again."

Matt shook his head at Jason and Creed's snickering. "She says this every day, and then every night she's back in those sexy glasses and granny panties beggin' for the D."

A french fry splatted on his face, and Alyssa snorted a laugh. God, she loved Willa. The spunky Almost Alpha of the Gray Backs had been coaching her through some of the confusing bear stuff. Since Beaston had Turned Willa against her will, she had a good idea of what Alyssa had been going through and some great, if sometimes unhelpful, advice on how to keep Clinton's attention in the bedroom. One included eating copious amounts of green and orange M&M's for boob growth and horniness.

"Where's Clinton?" Harrison asked. He was leaning against the wall, sipping a beer and watching the television behind the bar. "The vote is going to be announced any minute."

Indeed, everyone from Damon's mountains was crammed into Sammy's Bar, and even the Keller family of the Breck Crew, but Clinton had been MIA all day. Alyssa was getting worried. "I don't know. He swore he would be here."

"He'll be here," Beaston murmured from where he was patting Weston's little back against his shoulder. His little raven boy was dressed in a onesie that made him look like a cute little worm, compliments of Willa. Aviana was sipping a screwdriver and smiling tenderly at her boys. Beaston's eyes blazed that unsettling green, but he looked calm enough.

If Beaston said it, Clinton would be here in time, but as Alyssa looked around the bar at the crews all murmuring nervously, she couldn't help but wonder if Clinton would show up after the vote announcement.

When the door flung open, Clinton stood there, chest heaving, a look of panic on his face. He searched the room until he locked eyes on her.

Huffing a sigh of relief, she wound through the crowd and rested her forehead against his chest as he hugged her tightly. "Where have you been?"

"Picking them up." Clinton moved out of the way and gripped her shoulder, angling her toward the opening door.

A couple of familiar faces appeared, and a shocked noise wrenched out of Alyssa's throat. "Mom? Dad?"

Their faces brightened, and Mom reached for her, hugged her up tight.

"What are you guys doing here?"

"We wanted to be here for the vote results. It's a big day for you and Clinton. No matter what happens, we'll be here for whatever support you need."

Alyssa hugged her dad and did her best to keep her tears inside. It meant so danged much that they were here. That Clinton had arranged this. She'd missed her parents since she'd moved to the Boarland Mobile Park.

"Quiet in the bar!" Kong yelled. He whistled a shrill sound that hunched all the shifters shoulders and had half of them cussing him out. "Sorry! It's on!"

He pushed the volume button on the television behind the bar with a yard stick as everyone surged forward.

Alyssa blew out a nervous breath. This was it. If this didn't go well, she and Clinton were still illegally paired, and she would have no shot at taking his last name or registering with the Boarlanders. So much work and rallying had gone into this moment that now felt surreal. As Clinton gripped her one hand, and her parents gripped the other, Alyssa bit her lip and sent up a silent prayer that the humans had done the right thing. She and the others had all voted, but there weren't that many of them. Not enough to sway a national vote. This one rested on the human's ability to be tolerant.

The news anchor droned on, building it up, and Alyssa looked up at Clinton. His eyes were steady on her. "It's okay," he murmured. "Even if they vote no, I'm still yours, and you're still mine. Always, okay?"

"Yeah."

"And the vote is…"

"I can't even watch." Alyssa squeezed her parents' and Clinton's hands and ducked her head, closed her eyes tight. *Please, please, please.*

The bar erupted in cheering, and she was jostled about. "Did it pass?"

Clinton was yelling, and his smile big.

"Did it pass?" she asked louder as Mom hugged her shoulders.

"Baby, they voted yes to reinstating the rights." Mom was crying hard, and even Dad was wiping his eyes. "You have your rights back. You all do."

Alyssa's face crumpled, and she let off a sob because she'd been so scared of more rallies and riots and prejudice, but the humans had come through for them. They'd come through! Proof there were more good people than bad in the world.

The bar went eerily quiet, and Denison Beck got on the microphone. "Y'all know tonight is huge for us. For our families, for our future." He lifted a glass of beer. "For Damon's mountains. But tonight isn't just about the vote."

Alyssa looked around, shocked that everyone had gone so quiet. She'd expected the cheering to last much longer.

Denison grinned at her. At her? "Beaston already told us we would win tonight."

"What?" She frowned at the expectant faces of her friends. "Why didn't anyone tell me?"

"Because this is a surprise party for you, Alyssa," Denison said. "Turn around."

Alyssa turned to Clinton, but he wasn't standing where he had been. He'd dropped to one knee, and he had a sparkling diamond ring offered up to her.

Alyssa covered her mouth to stifle her sobbing.

"I didn't Turn you right, and I'll always regret that, but I wanted to do this right. I wanted to propose to you like you deserve."

Clinton ghosted a grin at her dad. "I asked your dad for your hand in marriage, and he and your mom wanted to be here for your big day. My family, too."

Clinton's voice broke, and he jerked his head toward an older man and woman near the wall. They were surrounded by four giant men with sandy blond hair like Clinton's. His mom had her hands clasped in front of her mouth and tears streaming down her cheeks, and she waved at Alyssa and pressed her hand to her chest, like she was trying to keep her heart in there.

"We're legal to do what we want now," Clinton said, his eyes so raw, so adoring. "You can have whatever kind of wedding you want. Whatever makes you happy. I just want you for always. Bound to me, my mate, my wife, all of it. I've loved you since I was a kid. You were the steady good in my life, even when I thought I would never see you again." He blew out a shaking breath. "Alyssa?"

"Yes! Yes, yes, yes," she cried out, dropping down to hug him.

"Wait, woman!"

"I said yes. Yes."

Clinton settled her back on her feet as everyone was laughing and cheering and clapping around them. "Let me ask you!"

"Yes."

He chuckled and tried to give her a serious look that failed when his smile peeked through. "Will you marry me?"

"Yes!" Her hands were shaking so bad Clinton had to hold her hand steady to put the big ol' rock on the finger he'd turned green with his cheap promise ring so many years ago.

The bar erupted with cheering that rattled the walls and shook the floor beneath her feet. Her bear was still new and so overwhelmed right now. Clinton stood and hugged her, lifted her off the ground, and kissed her. She couldn't breathe with all this emotion roiling through her. She tried to control herself by laying little pecking kisses over his cheeks.

"Hey," Clinton murmured, easing back. "It's okay."

"I'm gonna Change." Her chest was constricting with the long snarl of her bear.

"No." He shook his head and smiled at her. "Look at me. Stay with me."

She dragged air in and nodded over and over as the crowd jostled them. And when she felt in control and smelled less like fur, Clinton set her down and handed her to Audrey, who was bawling even harder than Alyssa was.

And as she was passed from friend to friend for hugs and congratulations, Denison and Brighton Beck hit the first chord of a song and filled the bar with music. Kong and Layla were working hard behind the bar, and every single person in here donned happy smiles.

Her eyes locked on Clinton through the crowd as he talked with his family, and she made her way toward him. Toward her future.

The shifters of Damon's mountains were cheering and clapping behind her, where they would always be. They would always have her back and wouldn't let her fall. And Clinton would always be there, strong for her when she was weak, and she swore on everything she would be that for him, too, because after all he had gone through and sacrificed, he deserved to be okay.

Shifters had their rights back, and the future was bright, not only for her and Clinton, but for the children here. The ones who hid tiny owlets, ravens, bear cubs, and dragons inside of them.

And someday she would get to tell her and Clinton's cubs about their fight to find each other again and their journey to carve out this beautiful existence among these incredible people. These amazing people who had somehow transcended friendship and become family.

She stopped in front of Clinton and inhaled deeply. He smelled of happiness, and she'd never scented that on him before. Not like this.

"I have to tell you something," he said, pulling her waist to him.

She twisted her engagement ring around her finger and canted her head, mesmerized by that smile on his lips, the one she lived and breathed for. Slowly, she slid her arms over his shoulders and looked up into those blazing silver eyes. "Tell me."

The smile dipped slightly from his lips, but lingered in the corners. "I love you."

And there it was—her dandelion.

She wanted to cry and scream and celebrate. He'd been so brave with his admission, and now infinite joy filled the rest of the hole she'd been carrying in her middle.

Alyssa hugged him and nuzzled his face the way her bear told her to. "I love you, too, Clinton. More than anything. You're mine. My mate. My love." She smiled as he hugged her tighter, and she whispered softly against his ear, "You were always mine, and now look what you've given me."

She rested her cheek against his as they looked out over the shifters and humans celebrating the vote, celebrating their commitment to each other. Tagan, Creed, Harrison, Kong, Damon and Cody Keller stood near the bar, the alphas watching their people and talking to each other through happy smiles. Kids chased each other through the crowd, laughing freely. Alyssa's family and Clinton's family were hugging and talking with animated, happy faces. Willa was dancing on the bar in a plaid skirt and her black crop top with the cartoon worm. She was rubbing her round belly and waggling her eyebrows at Matt. Cora Keller and Beck were up there with her, too, dancing like a hundred pounds had been lifted off their shoulders with the results of the vote. On the dance floor, Beaston was swaying from side-to-side with Aviana and Weston. They were in the middle of a dozen other Ashe Crew, Gray Back Crew, Boarlander Crew, and Breck Crew couples. The Beck Brothers' were slaying a country song, and this was it. This was a moment that made a thousand lifetimes.

Alyssa smiled up at her mate. He wasn't Crazy Clinton anymore. He was just…Clinton.

He'd given her friends and family, filled

her hollow places, and loved her even when she didn't know who she was. He'd given her a crew she would do anything for and the beautiful sound of laughter that filled Sammy's Bar.

He'd given her the animal in her middle, and 1010, and a safe haven.

But most importantly, Clinton had fought to stay whole until they could find each other again. He'd given her his whole heart.

Alyssa didn't want to remember her past anymore. It didn't matter *how* she and Clinton found their happily ever after among the shifters in Damon's mountains.

It only mattered that they had.

Want More of the Boarlanders?

The Complete Series is Available Now

Other books in this series:

Boarlander Boss Bear
(Boarlander Bears, Book 1)

Boarlander Bash Bear
(Boarlander Bears, Book 2)

Boarlander Silverback
(Boarlander Bears, Book 3)

Boarlander Beast Boar
(Boarlander Bears, Book 4)

About the Author

T.S. Joyce is devoted to bringing hot shifter romances to readers. Hungry alpha males are her calling card, and the wilder the men, the more she'll make them pour their hearts out. She werebear swears there'll be no swooning heroines in her books. It takes tough-as-nails women to handle her shifters.

Experienced at handling an alpha male of her own, she lives in a tiny town, outside of a tiny city, and devotes her life to writing big stories. Foodie, wolf whisperer, ninja, thief of tiny bottles of awesome smelling hotel shampoo, nap connoisseur, movie fanatic, and zombie slayer, and most of this bio is true.

Bear Shifters? Check
Smoldering Alpha Hotness? Double Check
Sexy Scenes? Fasten up your girdles, ladies and gents, it's gonna to be a wild ride.

For more information on T. S. Joyce's work,
visit her website at
www.tsjoycewrites.wordpress.com

Made in the USA
Thornton, CO
02/23/23 19:25:18

ce459803-805a-44fb-8e1f-b53097b23347R01